His Challenging Lover

Elizabeth Lennox

CONTENTS

Chapter 1

Autumn stood by the side of the receptionist's desk, praying the woman wouldn't say the words that would once again break her heart. Just ask for any other name, she silently prayed. Any name, even someone who didn't work here would make her feel better.

Unfortunately, fate wasn't playing nice today.

"I'm here to see Xander Thorpe," the blond woman with the almost dripping red lips said while flicking her thick, blond hair back over her shoulder.

Autumn knew that the hair flip was only to show off her impressive bosom, perfectly displayed by the deep V of her red dress.

Diane, the receptionist, acted professionally, exactly as Autumn had trained her. She turned to her computer with a gracious smile, her fingers poised over the keyboard as she said, "Do you have an appointment?" Diane knew that her boss, the amazingly lovely brunette with the deep brown eyes, was standing beside her stiffly, watching to see how this exchange played out. And everyone knew that there was something going on between Autumn and the gorgeous Xander Thorpe, although none were entirely sure what that "something" was.

The blond bimbo, as Autumn now thought of the latest female intrusion, laughed and waved her hand. "I don't, but I'm pretty sure he'll see me," she said and smoothed her hands down her hips. "Just tell him Jessica is here to speak with him."

Diane knew the process. She typed the information into the computer, then sent off the notice to Xander's assistant, a new woman by the name of Tilly. She was a temporary employee, brought in yesterday when his last one quit without any notice. Xander had a bad habit of going through assistants at a horrible rate. With

1

gritted teeth, Autumn slapped the file folder down onto the table and walked quickly out of the area. Her feet pushed her faster, desperate to not see…

Unfortunately, Autumn didn't make her escape fast enough. When the woman in red entered Xander's office and closed the door, the jokes and money from the other staff members quickly started exchanging hands.

"How much did you win?" James, one of the third year lawyers asked another associate just as Autumn hurried past his desk.

Autumn gritted her teeth and shook her head, walking quickly by him but trying to paste a calm-looking smile on her face. As usual, wagers were being settled now that the previous girlfriend, a lovely brunette, had been replaced by the gorgeous blond. Autumn desperately didn't want anyone in the office to know how painful she found the betting. Xander's love life served as entertainment for the rest of the office, but it hurt her more than it should. Every time a new woman came into his life, Autumn hated Xander just a little bit more. Why should she even care who he dates? He could date anyone he wanted! She just wished he would keep his personal life outside the office.

Maybe that's what bothered her so much about his philandering ways. She hurried down the hallway, ignoring the laughter and money changing hands. It looked like a new pool was being set up. If Xander would keep his private life more private, it wouldn't bother her so much. She preferred efficiency and order, trained her support staff to work hard, look and act professionally and be exceptionally helpful and competent.effective. The bets about how long the current flavor-of-the-moment would last reduced everyone's productivity.

Autumn knew that the betting on Xander's love live occurred but she never participated. Everyone thought she was just being polite and trying to ignore her boss's dalliances. But she knew better why she wasn't delving into the bitter world of Xander's girlfriend office pool.

Axel and Ash were walking towards her and she quickly looked down. But Axel wasn't having any of that. He caught the flash of pain in her eyes and touched her arm gently, obviously concerned.

"What's going on, Autumn? You look like you've just lost your best friend."

Autumn laughed bitterly. "Oh, goodness, nothing so dramatic as that," she came back, her shoulders squared off against the pain ripping through her silly, vulnerable heart. "It's just the changing of the guard." At their blank looks, she sighed and said, "Xander's old girlfriend is out and a new one is in. Everyone in the cubicles is paying up on their bets and placing new wagers on this next woman." She was looking downwards, wishing she could just race to her own office and hide away until the pain abated, but then she caught the twenty dollar bill exchange from Axel to Ash. "That was thirty-one days, right?" he asked.

She nodded numbly, unaware that her mouth was hanging open in shock that even Xander's two younger brothers would be involved in the betting.

When those dratted tears threatened to spill over her lashes, she took a deep, frantic breath and started moving around the two extremely large men. "If you'll excuse me," she said, but didn't bother finishing the sentence as she raced down the hallway and into her office.

She wasn't aware of the two men staring after her, both of them frozen into stunned silence. "Well I'll be..." Axel said, watching until she slammed the door to her office.

Ash stopped staring at the now-closed door and grinned towards his brother. "I think that's another twenty you owe me," he said.

Axel looked at his brother, then back at the closed door one more time. "I would have sworn..." he started to say, then shook his head. "You were right." And he handed Ash another twenty. "At least it was just around us."

Ash nodded his head as well, his mouth grim with irritation over his older brother's insensitivity. "Yeah. She's usually more in control."

Axel grinned as they both turned to continue their walk down the hallway. "Want to bet on when he'll crack and admit it to her?"

Ash was already shaking his head. "Hell no! Big Brother Xander realizing what's going on?"

Both men laughed as they continued towards their destination, unaware of the woman leaning against the doorway fighting back the tears. Thankfully, Autumn didn't hear their conversation or she would have been even more humiliated. As it was, she just had to deal with the pain of seeing Xander with yet another beautiful woman. She hated this, she told herself, brutally wiping the tears from her cheeks. He was such a jerk! Why did he have to bring those women here? It was an insult to everyone's professionalism and productivity.

He should be more inconspicuous about his personal life during business hours, and he should never have his girlfriends trot around here like that! It was unprincipled and inappropriate!

And it hurt! Damn the man!

She sat down behind her desk and dropped her head onto her hands, trying to control the painful emotions that were threatening to choke her. She should find another job, she told herself firmly. She shouldn't put herself through the pain of watching him come and go with those women.

The idea of not being here, of not seeing...all the Thorpe brothers, caused another sharp stab of pain. She liked her job, except when there was a changing of the guard. She really shouldn't let it bother her so much. She should just look the other way and leave him to his philandering ways.

Or maybe she should talk to him, try and convince him to keep his lady loves outside the office. Too many staff members watched them come and go. Not to mention the younger men on the staff seeing ridiculous antics like that. Xander was a role model! He was teaching the younger men that women were disposable, that they weren't worth the effort to invest in a real relationship.

When the meeting notification pinged, she looked at her computer and sighed. She wouldn't have time to consider the option of finding a new job right at the moment. She had yet another meeting to attend. Thankfully this one was just with her own staff so she wouldn't have to sit at the conference table and feel Xander's presence. Or even worse, fight the growing anger whenever he prodded her temper. The man was ingenious about getting a rise out of her and no matter how hard she tried to stay calm, she inevitably ended up firing one or two pointed jibes his way just to get back at him. He changed her, she thought resentfully. He made her act in a petty manner and she hated it. She wanted to remain calm and unemotional, to appear professional at all times. But he just kept on pushing her buttons, making her angry and forcing her temper out into the open.

She took a deep breath and grabbed a tissue out of her drawer, patting down her cheeks. With efficient movements, she pulled a mirror out of another drawer and repaired her makeup, furious that he'd reduced her to tears this time. When her face looked calm once again, she stood up and walked to the window in her office, taking several deep breaths.

From the other side of the office, Xander watched with rising fury and frustration as Autumn Hallman walked into her office, closing the door. Closing everyone out. He saw his brothers turn the corner and he made a mental note to ask them later if they knew what had upset her. He would do it now, but he had to get rid of Jessica Lilsedale. The irritating woman had attached herself to his arm last night at some charity function and he hadn't been able to get rid of her. Why had she shown up here? He'd given her absolutely no encouragement last night. And now she wanted a private word with him?

He'd gotten into the office early this morning, needing time to get work done because he had a busy schedule. Normally, the fall was a slower than normal period in his division, but not this year for some reason. Business was thriving and he was going to have to bring on a few more lawyers if this pace kept up.

He ran the family law practice in The Thorpe Group, which included all family issues, but mostly it came down to the divorce division. He had a thriving practice with people almost lining up at the door wanting to tear apart the spouse that, only a few years earlier, they'd promised to love, honor and cherish. It always astounded him that people who had once claimed to love each other so much that they wanted to dedicate their lives together, could reduce their entire world down to money and a desire to hurt someone as painfully as possible, in any way available.

Jessica was rattling on and on about some inane issue. All the while, he was looking down the hallway towards Autumn's office door, willing her to come out and show her face just so he could see that she was okay. Had someone hurt her feelings? Was she overwhelmed with her work load? He'd go directly to his brothers if they were laying too much on her slender shoulders. She was just one woman, but she continued to accept more and more responsibility within the firm.

Good grief, what was Jessica prattling on about now?

"So what do you think?" she asked, tilting her head and twirling her bleached blond hair with her talon-tipped fingers.

Xander hadn't heard a word she'd said. "I'm sorry, what was the question?"

Jessica laughed and playfully punched his shoulder. "Tonight! The party? Are you up for some fun?"

Attending any social function with this annoying female was definitely not going to happen. With as much patience as he could muster, he walked the irritating woman to the elevators, ignoring her obnoxious chatter. "I'm sure you'll have a much better time without me," he said and took her hand, effectively releasing her grip on his arm. He lifted her hand to his lips and, as graciously as possible, kissed her fingers in an effort to send her off into the descending elevators.

As soon as she was gone, he breathed a sigh of relief. Unfortunately, the cloying cloud of perfume she left in her wake almost made him gag. Why did women insist on bathing in the rancid stuff? His mind instantly thought of the way Autumn smelled. She was always fresh and clean. He couldn't think of a single time that she'd worn perfume. But she always smelled…incredible.

Back in the office, he stood at the end of the hallway, contemplating Autumn's closed door. She was upset and he had no idea why but it tore him apart.

He had no right to feel this way. She was an employee, and an exceptional one at that. He was one of the owners, so he should remain distant and treat her just like he would any other employee. He and his three other brothers owned equal shares in The Thorpe Group and, between the four of them, they could cover about every area of law possible.

What he couldn't cover was his need to hold Autumn Hallman in his arms. Seeing her like this, her beautiful, brown eyes filled with tears, tore him apart. He hated seeing her in pain.

What could be wrong?

She'd been with the firm for five years, working here as a receptionist while still in college, and she'd become even more valuable as she'd matured. And more beautiful. He'd been aching for her ever since she'd first walked through the doors looking for a job, and that need had only intensified as he'd gotten to know her.

He knew that she thought of him as a royal pain in the ass. At times, he annoyed her just to see her brown eyes sparkle with anger and those pretty, pale cheeks bloom with color. And other times, he was in so much pain to possess her, to be with her and be near her that he snapped at the world. His administrative assistants bore the brunt of his irritation, but he couldn't deny the pleasure of working with Autumn every time he had to replace the previous assistant who had quit.

Of course, it helped that the last several assistants were completely inept. He wasn't one to pressure someone into quitting, just so he could have one-on-one time with Autumn. No, he'd never do that to his staff. The ones that had left over the past two years had genuinely been under skilled and possessed of a bad attitude.

The last one had quit just yesterday, but he didn't mind since he'd been about to fire her anyway. The client files were a complete mess and the woman had lost track of all of his appointments, triple scheduling clients and leaving large gaps in between.

But now he felt like someone was tearing off his arm – all because Autumn was upset about something. And she had to be genuinely upset because, unless she was snapping at him, she never let her emotions interrupt business. This was extremely unusual.

"Ms. Davenport is here to see you," his temporary assistant said, handing him the file.

Xander took the file with resignation. He wanted to toss the file into his office and storm down to Autumn's office so he could fix whatever had hurt her. Instead, he focused on his next client, reading through the file and skimming through the details. "She has coffee already?" Xander asked, distracted by the file and thinking about Autumn, worried that someone in the office might have hurt her feelings.

No, that was impossible. Besides him and his brothers, there wasn't anyone with as much authority in the office as Autumn. She ruled the schedules and the case loads with military precision. If anyone dared to irritate her, she quickly and efficiently put them in their place.

He loved hearing that too. When one of the other lawyers tried to get uppity, she'd simply give them a piece of her mind. Anyone who came up against the mighty Autumn Hallman went away with their tail between their legs.

Except him. He loved going head to head with her.

Unfortunately, he knew that Autumn wasn't interested in him. She had her own life, her own hobbies and plans for the future.

But he couldn't stop his eyes from looking at Autumn's closed door before he sighed and made his way into his own office. Ms. Davenport awaited. She was on her third marriage and each one made her wealthier than the last. With his help, of course.

CHAPTER 2

Autumn came into the office early the next day, needing to get some work done in the quiet time before the rest of the staff came into work. She couldn't believe the week she was having. First, her best friend gets arrested for murder and next, yet another assistant quits on Xander. That was the third one in six months! What does that man do that annoys them so much?

Okay, so the last one wasn't up to scratch. She was embarrassed to say it, but she'd known from the beginning that that one wasn't going to work out.

But in her defense, she had to work closely with Xander each time they hired a personal assistant for him. During that last round, she'd just short circuited the interview process because it was getting harder and harder to be around him. Keeping her distance was the most important way she kept her sanity while working so closely with him. Unfortunately, doing interviews for his assistant meant sitting next to him, feeling the man's heat emanating from his body even from the distance she maintained from him. She couldn't handle that for more than a few days so she'd convinced him that the last woman was good enough.

Now she had to pay the price for cutting the interview process short. She had to go through the whole process over again: sit next to him, listen to his teasing comments, and argue with him about one candidate or another.

It was an exhausting process.

She couldn't understand why even her office had to be so close to his. It was like the man invented ways to torture her.

But of course, he couldn't know how she felt about him. To the rest of the office, she and Xander were combatants with brief periods of peaceful coexistence. Lately though, those peaceful periods were few and far between. They had been snapping at each other more often lately and, although at times it was exhilarating, she had to admit that it sometimes became exhausting.

Especially when one of his lady loves came to pick him up for their date.

She truly hated the man during those periods. It wasn't even that the man had a type! He dated redheads, blonds, brunettes. He escorted celebrities, famous actresses, social butterflies and power-hungry career women.

With a sigh, she wiped her eyes and shook her head. "Enough!" she told herself firmly. "The day marches on!" And so would she.

She turned around and looked at her computer. She had numerous issues to deal with and not much time to finish them. She was worried about her friend Mia who was battling murder charges, but every time she asked Ash about her, he just told her that he had everything under control. She had to trust him on that. And if anyone could get Mia out of that mess, it would be Ash. He was brilliant.

Mia would be in the office again today, answering more questions from Ash and his team. Maybe the two of them could catch a movie tonight, escape from the pressure of Mia's murder charges and Autumn's irritating boss.

She sighed and slid her chair under her desk, losing herself in the latest plans to make the law firm more efficient. Once again, she lost track of time as one issue after another cropped up during the morning. She loved her job, loved the way people relied on her to smooth out the troubles. Fixing things was her forte and she thrived on finding good solutions to every problem and keeping The Thorpe Group organized.

When she finally realized how hungry she was, it was past the normal lunch period. She grabbed her wallet and headed outside, raising her face up to the warm sunshine. There wouldn't be too many more days like this, she thought. The days were already shorter and there was a definite bite to the night time air. Winter was coming quickly.

Despite the later hour, the lunch crowd at the building deli was heavy and Autumn sighed as she waited at the end of the line. This deli was always crowded but it also had the best sandwiches at a reasonable price for several miles. They made some sort of sauce that added a zing and a zip, making the whole experience much more enjoyable. No one knew what that sauce was, but several people had tried. Occasionally there were recipes in the office kitchen where someone thought they might have figured out the recipe. No one had discovered the formula exactly though so the mystery remained.

Normally, she would have called in her order and had it waiting at the checkout line, a great service the deli provided. But it had been too busy today in the office. And because she'd had trouble falling asleep last night, worrying about Mia and Xander and wondering what he might be doing, she'd woken up too late to grab something for breakfast. So here she was, waiting impatiently for her chance to order a sandwich.

She glanced across the street, considering just grabbing a yogurt at the small convenience store. It would certainly be faster, but at that moment, the line moved forward and she stuck with her desire for a filling, spicy sandwich.

"Hey!" a voice called out from somewhere to the left of her. She glanced in that direction, but she was too hungry to give it much thought.

Suddenly, the crowd parted and she saw what was happening. And couldn't believe her eyes!

"Get the hell out of the way, lady!" a brutish, bullish man was saying to an elderly woman wearing sensible shoes and a warm cardigan even on the warmish October day. Her grey hair looked frazzled and her eyes nervous as she watched the man with the fuzzy mustache warily.

Another man, this one thinner and taller, shook his head. "She was in line first," the stranger said in a placating tone, but even he didn't want to confront the portly blowhard.

"Oh yea?" the man taunted, his eyes narrowing and his hands balling into fists. "Well, prove it!" he snapped and started forward. His intent was clear and everyone around scattered, pushing backwards to avoid getting caught in the fight.

The horrible man swung out, his hand missing the thin gentleman but side striking the elderly lady who went down with the initial bump. Her cry of fright was heard by one and all but no one stepped forward to intervene.

A small part of Autumn's mind was still functioning properly and told her to stay out of it. But the other part of her brain, the part that wasn't functioning rationally and was outraged that someone would hit an elderly person, was in control and she was livid that this man had hurt someone who was just standing, waiting for lunch. Instead of pushing back into the crowd, she stepped forward, her instincts made her grab onto the fat man's arm. Unfortunately, she realized too late that the arm wasn't just lard, but packed with muscles. But by the time she realized that, he was already turning around to confront his newest threat.

Autumn dropped the man's arm and stood with her feet braced apart, her hands at the ready, trying to anticipate what the burly man might do next. "Call the police," she ordered to the crowd. Not to anyone in particular, and she knew that the police wouldn't be able to get here in time to save her but she threw that out as a threat anyway, hoping the man would stop and think. It might even give her a tiny reprieve, enough to slow him down.

No such luck. The call for the police only enraged the man further. That rational part of her mind, the part that wasn't blanking out with the anger over what this man had done, noticed all the other men and women standing back, their mouths open and their eyes wide with amazement of all that was unfolding. It flashed through her mind that, if everyone put their efforts together, they could stop this man simply by grabbing his arms and pinning him to the ground.

But obviously no one was thinking clearly. Not even her. And the man rushed her, his fist swinging out and clipping her under her jaw while his other hand swung out and aimed for her ribs. She gasped at the pain, twisted slightly and used the man's momentum to throw him off balance. He came back at her in only seconds, not giving her enough time to regroup. As she stared at the bloodlust in his eyes, she knew that the previous tackle was only a precursor to this one but she spun around and braced herself, prepared to do whatever it took to stop this man.

All she saw was him coming towards her one moment and the next, he was gone, slammed up against the wall of the deli with his arm twisted behind his back and his right cheek smashed so he wasn't able to look anywhere but up at the ceiling.

"So, you like taking swings at women half your size, eh?" Xander was saying, twisting the man's arm slightly and causing him to flinch again. "How about if you take on someone a bit bigger and see how you fare?" he asked.

There was applause all around but Autumn only saw Xander's enormous, magnificent body as he glared down at the portly man. She knew she should hide her appreciation for his tall, muscular form, but it was simply too impressive.

There was another commotion over by the doors as the police belatedly arrived, hands on their pistols as they quickly surveyed the situation. When they saw who was holding the man, both police officers' jaw dropped.

"Are you okay, Mr. Thorpe?" one of them asked, rushing over with his handcuffs in his hand, efficiently taking over the man being restrained.

"I'm fine. But this man assaulted the lady on the floor and Autumn Hallman, my office manager."

The police officer was more than a little overwhelmed by the idea of talking to Xander Thorpe. He was sort of a legend in the boxing ring as well as the legal community. But the officer squared his shoulders, eager to look good in front of the man most officers revered. "We'll book him for assault and battery as well as disorderly conduct," the other officer said. He went over to the elderly woman, helping her stand up and checking her to see if she needed an ambulance. Meanwhile, Xander spun around to glare at Autumn and she cringed at the furious look in his indigo blue eyes. Why was he angry with her?

Okay, so that was a silly question. Xander was always angry with her for one reason or another. And normally, she would spit the fire right back at him, giving as good as she got. But she'd never seen him this furious. Normally, he reserved his anger to sarcastic, pithy comments in a meeting or biting remarks when she didn't find him a staff addition or replacement quickly enough.

This was a whole new level of fury.

With the police officers trying to organize the witnesses, get statements and haul the brute away, Xander walked slowly towards her. Actually, it wasn't so much walking as it was stalking. There were only about five steps separating both of them, but it seemed like a lifetime for him to reach her. When he was less than an inch away from her, she looked up into his blue eyes, her neck craning back because she couldn't move backwards and he wasn't relenting.

He didn't say a word. He simply grabbed her arm in a vicelike grip and hauled her out of the deli.

"We're going to need Ms. Hallman to give us a statement," one of the officers was saying as Xander dragged her to the doorway.

Autumn scrambled to keep up but it was hard because the Xander was so much taller than she was. Well, and she was wearing three inch heels. She knew they made her legs look awesome, but they didn't make running too easy.

"I'll bring her to you later," Xander replied to the officer as politely as his anger would allow.

Autumn was about to demand an explanation but he didn't stop long enough for her to even get a breath. This man had tormented her for years with his anger and she was sick of it! It was going to end today! She was just about to pull her arm free and confront the man when he pulled her to the side of the building.

Xander didn't even try to get control of his anger. He'd never been so terrified in his life as when he saw Autumn confront that ridiculous excuse for a human being. And when the man had actually hit her, marred her perfect, beautiful skin, he'd seen red. There had been no conscious thought after that. It was pure instinct. With a rage surging through his blood, he'd grabbed the man before he could harm Autumn again, moments before he was about to make contact in his second charge, and slammed the man against the wall. With a vicious twist, Xander had pulled the man's arm behind his back, wanting desperately to snap the arm off of him. He'd glanced back, catching sight of Autumn again. Seeing her, knowing that she was once again safe, was the only thing that gave him back some measure of control.

When the police arrived, he was more than happy to release the dung heap to them but he still couldn't rid himself of the fury and fear. With a growl and a determination to ensure that Autumn, his Autumn, his beautiful, delicate, sweet and overly brave Autumn, was okay, he grabbed her arm. He wasn't sure what he was going to do. All he knew was that he had to ensure that she was okay. That she was still whole.

When he saw the side of the building, out of the way of other people passing by, he hauled her there. He'd thought he was only going to confront her, demand an explanation as to why she'd taken such ridiculous risks with her life and her body. But instead, he found himself kissing her. But this wasn't just a kiss. This was a life affirming, knee bracing, stomach clenching demonstration of all that he felt for this woman.

Autumn was so surprised when his mouth covered hers that she was stunned motionless for all of about one eighth of a second. And then her mind realized that Xander was kissing her. No, not just kissing her. His body was pressing against hers, his hips were grinding into hers, his hands were sliding up against her body…underneath her silk blouse no less…and she couldn't stop the immediate and overwhelming lust that surged through her. She wasn't just going to take this kiss. She gave back, demanding more, her hands sliding up his arms, feeling those bulging muscles underneath the deceptively tame dress shirt until she felt the heat of his skin on his neck. Pausing, she reveled in that heat, her fingers absorbing the texture before they moved higher, her fingers discovering that his hair was so soft, so silky. It was probably the only part of this man that was soft and she couldn't believe how good he felt, how incredible he tasted. She wanted this man like nothing she'd ever experienced in her life. She wanted him more than she'd ever thought possible.

And then he pulled back!

Her eyes looked up at him, surprised and confused. Her lips were aching for more, to feel Xander's firm lips against hers, taking and tasting and giving.

Why did he stop? Why was he doing this to her? Didn't he realize what he'd stirred inside of her?

When the wonderful, tantalizing heat of him pulled slightly away and her mind wasn't occupied by his mind-blowing kiss, her ribs suddenly started hurting. She tried not to cringe, but she must have failed because his eyes narrowed and he pulled away so he could look down at her.

"You're hurt!" he snapped, his breath hissing through his teeth as he bent lower, examining her cheek and jawline which were just starting to show signs of the blow she took.

"I'm fine," she whispered but his hands shifted slightly and she let out a small cry of pain.

His lips compressed as he looked down at her, that same fury breaking through the thick haze of lust. "You aren't fine," he contradicted, his fingers deftly feeling her ribs. When she cringed again, he shook his head. "I'm taking you to the hospital," he told her.

She shook her head. "No! No hospital!" she told him firmly. Her mother had died in a hospital and, in her mind, they were intricately, irrationally, woven into her psyche as buildings of death.

"You need to see a doctor," he told her firmly. "And probably an x-ray for your ribs."

"My ribs are fine," she stated emphatically, her fingers grabbing onto his forearm to keep him from doing something cruel, like taking his warm hand away from her skin that suddenly knew what his touch was like. "Just bruised. I'll be fine." To prove it, she held her breath, wondering if his fingers would move that small, fraction of an inch higher. Her breasts wanted that movement so badly, her mind shattering at the idea of his thumb, which was resting just below her breast, to move higher. Her nipple was already pebbled in anticipation but she couldn't say anything, couldn't beg him to finish what he'd just started.

They stared at each other for a long moment, the air crackling between them with the electricity sparking between their bodies. She couldn't breathe, she couldn't move. Nothing in the world made sense except for this man's hand to slide higher, to cover her breast and show her what his heat would feel like.

When he shifted his hand just slightly, she couldn't hide the pain that shot through her.

Xander said something under his breath that was unrepeatable then stepped back. "You're going to the hospital."

He started to take her hand and pull her towards his car, but she pulled right back. "Please," she begged, her eyes revealing the fear she felt towards hospitals. "I'll soak in a hot bath and everything will be fine," she promised. "Just no hospital."

"You need to see a doctor," he argued right back.

A doctor was better, but she'd rather just stay away from all of it. Her philosophy about sickness in the past had been to ignore everything. So far, it had worked out well enough. "If I don't feel better tomorrow, I promise to see my doctor."

Xander knew she'd be better off if she saw a doctor now, but he couldn't ignore the pleading look in those lustrous, brown eyes. He'd seen that stubbornness before and knew she wouldn't budge on the subject. Leaning down, his arms braced on the building behind her on either side of her head, he said, "Fine, you'll soak in a hot tub and relax for the rest of the afternoon. Otherwise, I'm taking you to the hospital and I'll tie you down to the x-ray machine if I have to. And I'll do that anyway if the hot bath doesn't help." He relented slightly, his hand reaching out and gently touching her cheek, cradling her head in his large, strong hand. "I promise I won't let anything happen to you at the hospital if it comes to that," he said with a deep, husky voice.

When he turned all sweet and gentle on her, Autumn's heart swelled with something she refused to identify. She didn't know how to deal with a kind Xander. She was so used to going head to head with him on every issue that this new Xander was a mystery. And so were the feelings that threatened tears to well up in her eyes.

She blinked rapidly, trying to hide her vulnerability from him. She didn't understand what she was feeling and it scared her.

"Come along," he said, still with that soft, gentle voice. He took her hand and led her through the back of the building to the parking garage. With a click, he unarmed his black, sleek sedan and opened the passenger side door for her.

"I can drive…"

"Get in, Autumn," he interrupted. It was firm, but still with that gentle, coaxing, you're-not-getting-out-of-this tone.

With a sigh, she slipped into the soft leather seat, amazed at how luxurious the car felt as it hugged her body. She didn't have time to think more about that though because a second later, Xander was getting in next to her, his long legs coming precariously close to her thighs. The car might be a luxury sedan, but Xander was an extremely large man and there rarely was a space big enough to contain him. Whatever room he was in, it always felt small to her. His shoulders were huge, his muscles bulged everywhere on his body and his legs were so long they ate up the distance between point A and point B. It was awesome when point A was her office door and point B was her desk. Every time he entered her office, her eyes were drawn to his legs, her mouth going dry as she watched those muscles bulge underneath his hand-tailored slacks.

"Where are we going?" she asked, swallowing the nervousness that suddenly sprang up with his nearness.

"I'm taking you home," he told her, his long, lean fingers deftly handling the steering wheel and Autumn was mesmerized by those fingers, her mind imagining what they looked like when they were examining her ribs, wondering what they would look like against her pale skin.

She took a deep breath and tore her eyes away, looking out the window instead. "Thank you for your help," she said.

Xander heard the wobble in her voice and realized that reaction was slowly setting in. The adrenaline was ebbing away and she would start to become exhausted pretty quickly.

"You're welcome," he said, then had to shake his head at the memory of her standing in front of that little lady, protecting her while confronting the furious man. "Why did you do it?" he asked, turning left and then right.

She might be looking out the window but she wasn't watching the landscape. She was thinking back to the point in the deli when the man had become belligerent, her mind starting to go over everything that happened. "I don't know. No one else was going to help those two. Someone had to do it."

He glanced down at her slender legs, demurely crossed at the ankles and her hands clenched in her lap. "So you stepped up and showed him who was boss." He chuckled at the way she'd stood, those sexy, three inch heels braced shoulder width apart in perfect fighting stance and her arms held out from her body, fists raised as if her hundred and twenty pound figure could stop a two hundred and fifty pound raging bull.

Autumn blushed at the memory. "Okay, so you were the one who showed him who the boss was. It was pretty amazing of you, how you stepped in and stopped him cold."

"My brothers and I spar in the ring." He looked down at her briefly, but she got the message. He was clearly stating that he was trained to step in and do something like that. She wasn't.

She bit her lip and looked out the window, feeling teary eyed and embarrassed by it. "I wasn't going to let that woman be hurt by that man."

"Admirable. Brave," he said with a nod, "but also stupid. You could have been seriously hurt."

"But I wasn't," she said simply, ignoring the pain that was starting to throb in her jaw and her ribs. She'd never admit to him how hard the man had punched her. She could deal with this, she told herself silently.

He took a deep breath as the anger started to well up inside him again. "This time. Promise me that you won't ever do something like that again."

She bit her lip and looked to the right, out the window. "I promise I won't do anything that I think is stupid."

He cursed under his breath, fighting to control his anger again. "Which leaves open a great deal of what I think might be stupid," he said, completely understanding what she was telling him.

He pulled into a parking garage and swung immediately into a space. "Come on," he said and turned off the engine.

Autumn was already out of the car before she realized that this wasn't her house. This wasn't even her neighborhood. Even if she'd saved her entire salary for the rest of her life, she'd never be able to afford just the smallest apartment in this neighborhood. "Where are we?" she asked.

"My place. I'm going to make sure you take care of yourself," he said and put a hand to the small of her back to guide her over to the elevators.

Autumn's heartbeat picked up, going triple time at the idea of entering Xander's space. She didn't even enter his office, standing in the doorway when she needed to talk to him about any subject. There was no way she was going into his private dwelling space. If his office was too personal, she couldn't even imagine what she would feel entering his apartment.

"I should just go home," she said quickly, starting to turn around. She intended to get a cab that would take her to her house so she could hide away, fearful about being alone in Xander's home. The alone part was the main worry, but there was also the idea of being surrounded by things that were all "Xander". It was hard enough being around him.

But Xander wasn't having that at all. "Come along," he countered and wrapped his arm around her waist, careful not to touch the bruise on her ribs. "You'll be fine. I won't let anything harm you."

She went, but only because her knees were shaking so badly that she couldn't stop their momentum towards the elevators. She stepped into the elevator and moved away from Xander, but he was still too close and too big. Just like in a conference room or back in his car, the man took up the space, filling every air particle with his maleness.

When the doors opened, he put that strong arm around her waist again, leading her into the apartment. She didn't even get a chance to look around, he nudged her right into a fabulous bedroom and then into a large, marble bathroom with steel and chrome everywhere. And a giant, soaking tub complete with jets. Her eyes bulged at such luxury and she couldn't stop the enormous sigh at the idea of soaking in that giant marble tub.

He heard her sigh and chuckled softly. "I'm glad there's finally something about me that you approve of."

She kept her mouth shut while he bent over and turned on the water, thinking that she definitely approved of his butt. It was a very nice butt, outlined by the stretched fabric of those slacks and her mouth went dry once again. Her eyes couldn't pull away and she wasn't aware that he added something to the water, causing bubbles to rise up as the water quickly filled the tub.

He turned around and caught her blushing, but didn't understand it. "I'll get you something for the pain. Get in the tub and relax."

She thought she might have nodded, but she wasn't completely sure. She was too stunned, frightened and her mind was frozen. She couldn't react, unable to believe that she was actually standing in Xander's luxurious bathroom.

The door clicked closed behind her but she still stared at the tub that was quickly filling up with bubbles and water. The lure was too much for her aching body to resist. With shaking fingers and quick looks behind her, she slipped her clothes off, folding them quickly and hiding her lacy underwear. Her eyes watched the inviting water, her body now desperate for the relief that hot water might offer.

There were steps getting up to the raised tub and even steps descending down the other side. It was huge! And amazing! It was set in the corner of the bathroom and the windows overlooked the city, revealing the Chicago River and all the skyscrapers and highways as people moved about the city.

She slid into the hot, scented water, closing her eyes as the heat spread through her whole body, making the aches quickly disappear, at least for the moment. Leaning back, she was amazed at how wonderful the marble contoured to her body, relaxing her back and her legs. It was possibly the most comfortable tub she'd ever lain in, but that wasn't really saying much since the only types of tubs she'd had the privilege to luxuriate in were the regular hardware store tubs that were more suitable to washing little kids than soaking an adult body. Her own townhouse was nice, perfect for her needs, except for the utilitarian bathrooms.

With a sigh, she allowed her body to relax, her eyes closed and her mind drifted back to that kiss on the side of the building. For the moment, she didn't try and figure out why she'd allowed Xander to kiss her, or why she'd even reacted to his kiss. She'd seen the women who paraded into the office to meet him. The man escorted a different woman every month around town to the fabulous, glamorous parties and social functions. The lucky ones lasted maybe five weeks, the boring ones perhaps only three. One lucky woman had been able to hang onto his interest for a record six weeks.

Not that she noticed how long each of them was able to last in Xander's arms. It wasn't that she was trying to measure how long each of them lasted, but it was hard not to when they were so frequent.

Besides, the other people in the office had bets going on how long each would last so it was hard to miss the office talk or the office pool that was taped to the freezer door in the office kitchen.

She shivered involuntarily at the thought of her co-workers betting on how long she could keep his interest. Not that she would even try. The man was an absolute jerk!

She couldn't blame him though. He saw the worst in relationships. In a very basic sense, his job was to tear up a marriage, dissect it to pieces and get the most from the relationship for one or the other person. He saw not only the worst part of a marriage; he saw the evilness and maliciousness of each person. Not only his client, either the wife or the husband, but sitting across the table, he also witnessed the worst in the opposite party. The fights that erupted occasionally were vicious as the hurt feelings poured out in every way possible.

Perhaps she should be nicer to him, more considerate. The man saw the bad in so many people; he shouldn't have to see it in the people he worked with.

Maybe she should move her office to another floor. She didn't need to be on his floor, she thought as she mentally reviewed the four floors and their layouts. Whenever they'd expanded their presence in the building, it was her job to assign office space to all the lawyers and support personnel. She'd always, for some inexplicable reason, kept her own office on the same floor as Xander.

Well, one time after a particularly frustrating week, she'd shuffled things around and was going to move her office to Ryker's area. But that move had been vetoed. She didn't understand all the details, but she hadn't fought the change at the time.

Maybe it was now time to move to a new area, get away from him a bit more. The man could probably use her office to hire another lawyer. He had more than seventy divorce attorneys under his domain across the country with more than thirty of them here in the Chicago office. It always amazed her how many people were dissolving their marriage but his business was thriving.

She turned off the water, reveling in the silence as the ache in her ribs slowly receded even more. Xander had been right. A hot bath was exactly what she'd needed. And she probably would have ignored the idea if she'd gone home. She most likely would have pulled out her computer and worked on the millions of issues that required her attention every day.

Yes, this was perfect, she thought with a thrill. Autumn had to keep reminding herself that she wasn't excited because it was Xander's bathroom. It was simply because she was relaxed for the first time in….months.

Not really relaxed. No, what she was feeling wasn't in any way relaxed. Rejuvenated. Yes, that was the word. She felt rejuvenated by the water and the bubbles. It was probably the lavender scented bubbles he'd provided for her.

It suddenly occurred to her – why did Xander have lavender scented bath bubbles? He hadn't even needed to search for them. That feeling of happiness quickly dissipated and something new and angry emerged within her even as the bubbles popped and deflated.

Suddenly, the door to the bathroom opened up and Xander stood there, his indigo blue eyes glared at her. "You kissed me back!" he growled.

Gone were the thoughts about who had brought the bubbles into his place and her mouth went dry at the memory of that kiss. That one, incredible, passionate and mind blowing kiss.

She started to shake her head but he strode over to the edge of the bathroom, his hands fisted on his hips and he barely stopped when he was right next to the bathtub. "Yes, you kissed me right back."

With that, he reached down and lifted her up, the water streaming down her body, bubbles floating around in non-strategic places. "Why did you respond to me?" he said, but he didn't wait for an answer.

His kiss made her toes curl. She didn't have time to be embarrassed that she was completely naked, nor did she have time to caution him that she was dripping wet. It barely even registered that he'd taken off his suit jacket and tie at some point. All she knew was that his strong arms were wrapping around her and he was once again kissing her. Those shocking feelings of desire, which had been suppressed on the short drive from the office to his apartment building fired right back to life and she was shivering in reaction.

She wasn't aware of her arms wrapping around his neck but she shivered with need when his own hands moved from her arms down her back, cupping her bottom and pulling her hips against his own. She couldn't seem to get enough of the man, her body pressing closely, her mind not even trying to understand what was happening as everything in her dealt with the surging, pounding, unrelenting need that was centered down low in her belly.

When he tore his mouth away, she cried out in protest but he ignored that and lifted her into his arms, straight up into the air. She looked down and just about melted when his mouth covered her nipple. She didn't realize that her legs wrapped around his waist or anything else. Time, business, responsibility…they were all suspended as she let her head fall backwards, the ache increasing as his mouth sucked hard on her breast, teasing then gentling before increasing the pressure again. When he moved his mouth to the other breast, she thought she might just melt into a puddle of desire.

He wasn't giving her any time to process, to even reciprocate. His arms lowered her back down and she kissed him back, her whole body trying to figure out what to do and how to manage what he was making her feel. But it was pointless. His hands were everywhere, finding places on her body she didn't even know had nerve endings. It seemed that everywhere he touched just made that horrible and wonderful ache intensify.

The cold on her back was her only moment of sanity but that was obliterated when she felt him slide into her heat. She had no memory of her fingers pulling, practically ripping his clothes off or of him grabbing his wallet and sheathing himself with protection. She only knew that, for a fraction of a second when he was finally naked and their bodies could touch without the hindrance of clothing, she felt satisfied. That moment in time disappeared the moment he moved against her, her skin firing in so many places and the need was driving her out of her mind. When his body shifted, she cried out. The ache soothed slightly and she shifted to take in more of him. She didn't know that her nails were digging into the skin on his shoulders. All she knew was that she wanted this feeling to continue, and she wanted to find something to soothe that ache.

When she felt the slight pain, she ignored it and moved her hands lower against his back to pull him deeper. When he was fully embedded inside of her, she smiled with exhilaration.

But then he started moving and that ache was almost painful. She couldn't handle this and her head slashed back and forth, her hips moving up to meet his thrust while her hands shifted downwards, her fingers pushing against his hips, encouraging him to move faster.

When her world splintered apart, she gasped and screamed out, clinging to Xander, not exactly sure how to deal with the wave after wave of pleasure his body was creating within her but enjoying the ride regardless.

Xander felt her climax and watched with fascination. He controlled his own release, wanting her to enjoy this to the fullest. But as her body writhed underneath him, he couldn't hold back any longer and he poured himself out, gritting his teeth with the most intense, most amazing climax he'd ever experienced.

He almost collapsed on top of her, but at the last moment, remembered her tender ribs and he rolled over. The cold tiles underneath his back startled him but then his fingers found her hair and he played with the soft tendrils, reveling for a long moment in the thrill that Autumn was here and he had just made love to the most perfect female he'd ever met.

Autumn gasped when she felt him shift their positions but she couldn't work up enough energy to protest. So when she found herself draped over his muscular chest instead of underneath him, she could only lay there, trying desperately hard to catch her breath.

She shivered when she felt his hands move down her back and smiled while her own fingers tangled in the light dusting of hair on his chest. But then she felt something lower and her eyes widened. She lifted her head slightly, looking up at him and almost laughed at his tight jaw.

She shifted slightly, feeling him fill her up once again and she gasped, shifting her hips slightly.

"Don't do that!" he growled and tried to hold her hips still.

Autumn closed her eyes and pushed against his chest. "Why not?" she asked, her body trembling all over again.

Xander's hands slid up her body, cupping her breasts from this vantage point. "Because if you don't, we're going to start all over again," he said with a husky growl.

She was fascinated. Shifting slightly, she gasped when she felt those quivers all over her body. "Wow,' she sighed and closed her eyes. Her head fell back slightly and she braced her hands on his stomach, shifting one more time. She definitely liked this position, having heard about it from others and read about it in books. Although she needed a much more detailed analysis of this position versus the last one to fully gauge which one was better.

She inhaled sharply when she felt his hands on her hips, bringing her down hard on his erection. Her mouth formed an "O" of surprise, not sure how anything so invasive could feel so…amazing!

"Do that again," he growled.

Autumn lifted her hips again, feeling the friction and shuddering at all the tingles that centered right down there on her body and radiated outwards. "Yes," she sighed.

"Damn it, Autum," he groaned. "You've got to move, honey."

She bit her lip, continuing the slow pace so she could feel all of him, absorb every sensation. She liked this. A lot! Ignoring him, she moved however she wanted, grabbing his hands away from her hips when he tried to make her move the way he wanted her to. She looked down at him, her eyes dilated, her body undulating against his and Xander laid his head back against the bathroom tiles and let her have her way. He enjoyed the view even though he thought he might die a slow death at the way she was moving, so slowly and her body trembling so beautifully.

With each press of her hips, she took him higher and higher. Xander tried very hard to restrain himself, finding a thrill in watching her discover her body, but after several minutes of this slow torture, he couldn't take it any longer. Lifting himself up so she was basically sitting in his lap, his mouth latched onto her nipple, sucking hard, then laving it with his tongue before doing it again and moving to the other one. Her cries egged him on and he grabbed her hips with his hands and took control of the pace. Lifting her up and pressing into her, he kissed her breasts at the same time that her climax caused her to scream out, her body both writhing to get away from him and demanding that he continue until she sagged against him. It took him only a few more strokes before he found his own climax and he fell backwards onto the bathroom tiles, once more replete as he held this incredible woman in his arms.

CHAPTER 3

Autumn looked around, stunned by the dim light starting to come through the windows. Xander hadn't bothered to close the blinds to his bedroom last night but she hadn't really given him a chance. She sighed and tried to bury her face in the pillow beside her. She might be alone in the bed, but she could still feel his heat all over her body. Even as exhausted as she was right at the moment, she still wanted to find him and kiss him, feel his hands all over her once again. She'd never experienced anything like that before. The way she felt when he touched her was nothing short of....electric.

She heard the shower running and knew she should get out of here. She wasn't sure what his reaction would be in the daylight, but she was a coward and didn't want to face him. Not after everything they'd done last night.

She sat up, holding the sheet in front of her. She bit her lip when she looked over and saw her clothes draped against one of the chairs. She'd been so careful to fold them up with her underwear hidden away. But now her lacy underwear and bra were dramatically draped on top of her clothes.

Autumn knew that her face was blushing even though he wasn't here to see it. She slid out of bed, in a panic now to get out of his bedroom before he finished with his shower. She didn't really understand why she didn't want to face him. They probably should talk about what had occurred, but she simply couldn't do it right now.

She pulled on her clothes in record time, then cursed when she realized that she didn't have her wallet. She must have lost it in the deli yesterday when the fight had broken out. She was about to burst into tears at the thought of seeing Xander this morning but then she spotted his wallet.

As she carried her shoes, she walked over to the wallet. Good grief, the man carried about three hundred dollars in his wallet. Who did that? Well, obviously the uber-wealthy did that. Xander clearly fell into that category.

She didn't have time to think about that. She grabbed a ten, wrote him a quick note telling him that she owed him the money, and then scampered out of the gorgeous place. When she stepped out of his apartment and there was only one apartment and the elevator door, she wondered about that, but didn't have time. She had to get out of there, panic setting in at the idea of seeing Xander this morning. She'd have to face him later, surely he'd be at the office, but that would give her an hour or two to figure things out without him close by, filling her nostrils with his spicy, male scent that was so incredibly tempting.

Damn! She rushed out of the building and raised her hand high, relieved a cab was just letting someone off. Thankfully, Xander lived right in the heart of the city which had a surplus of cabs available.

She jumped into the back of the cab and gave her address, then realized she didn't have keys or anything so she changed her mind and asked the driver to take her to the office. He didn't like that as much since it was a much shorter fare, but she didn't have time to worry about the feelings of the driver.

At the office, she ignored the curious stares of the receptionist and a few other early bird lawyers and hurried to her office. There she grabbed her keys and purse, still not sure where her wallet was. But she didn't care either. She raced home, fighting tears of confusion, bewilderment. How could she have fallen into bed so easily with Xander? They'd been duking it out about every issue ever since she'd started here.

Actually, that wasn't true really. The first year she'd been here, she'd taken the receptionist job while in college, thinking it would just be a temporary position until she found something in her field of business administration. Xander had stopped by the front desk on numerous occasions, flirting with her outrageously, giving her small gifts for Christmas or her birthday, making sure she got all the vacation time she requested. He'd been very sweet that first year.

It had been when she'd gotten promoted to administrative assistant to Axel that he'd started to change. Even then, it hadn't been mean, just a bit more standoffish. She hadn't understood it at first, but it had hurt. She'd missed his smiles and those funny conversations. They were never about anything in particular but he'd always been very kind and sweet. And when she'd bought her condo, he'd made sure that Axel had taken care of all the legal issues for free.

She didn't understand it at first, his distance. But she'd slowly pulled back as well. Their flirty friendship had slowly gone from friendship to acquaintances and then to outright battles at times.

As she stepped into her shower, she had to be perfectly honest with herself. It hadn't always been his fault. She'd been hurt when he'd showed up with his girlfriends at work. So maybe she had been the first one to pull away.

But he had become nasty when she'd stopped by one night with a date to grab her coat after a spontaneous dinner. Ever since then, they'd been battling each other over every issue possible.

With a sigh, she stepped out of the shower and stood in front of her mirror. She'd have to hurry in order to make it to work on time but the sight of her chin, looking definitely purplish blue, was quit hideous! How could he have made love to her when she'd looked like this? How crazy! The lights must have been even dimmer than she'd realized.

She quickly applied a thick coat of makeup, not wanting to draw attention to her bruise. Her ribs were also a bit blue, but they could be covered up by her silk shirt and suit jacket. She'd just wear her jacket all day, not wanting to answer the numerous questions about yesterday's deli incident.

After skillful application, she was able to hide most of the bruise. If one knew to look, they could see the color but otherwise, it just looked like she was wearing a lot of makeup. That was unusual, but couldn't be helped. She had enough work to do to stay in her office most of the day and avoid people so that should cut down on the questions and curiosity a bit.

She made it to the office and pretended like nothing earth shattering had just happened the previous night.

"Xander Thorpe is looking for you," Diane said as soon as she walked through the entrance.

Autumn stopped, frozen in place. "Why?" she asked after a prolonged, odd look.

Diane was startled by Autumn's question. She struggled for an answer but in the end, she simply said, "I'm not sure. He didn't say but he's called me three times in the last half hour to see if you've arrived. Should I call and tell him that you're on your way to his office?" she asked, lifting the phone and looking at Autumn.

"No," she snapped, then shook her head, putting her hand to her forehead and telling herself to calm down. "No," she said again, but not in a panicked voice. "I'll go to his office as soon as I get settled in."

Diane put the phone down and Autumn raced to her own office. She closed the door, taking deep breaths as she leaned against the wood. She'd have to face him at some point. Better to just get it over with.

She put her purse down and tried to gather her strength. But the knock on the door had her spinning around, her eyes wide with fright.

Sure enough, Xander stood in the doorway looking huge and delicious. At the first sight of him, all she could think about doing was throwing herself into his arms again, asking him to kiss her like he'd done last night, make her feel those strange and amazing feelings once again.

But he looked wary, not exactly in the catching-a-woman mindset.

"You okay?" he asked, his dark blue eyes looking at her from the top of her head to her black, pointed heels. She wasn't positive, but she thought he might have paused as his eyes moved over her breasts. Please don't let him be wondering what her current underwear looked like, she thought feverishly.

"I'm fine," she said but couldn't hold his gaze.

"You left this morning," he came back after a long silence.

She bit her lip. "Yes. I'm sorry. I wasn't sure…what to…what you might think…what might…" she couldn't finish her statement. She wasn't really sure what she was thinking anyway.

"You weren't sure what I might say when I saw you in my bed? Or perhaps if you'd cared to join me in the shower?" he asked, his voice deep and sexy.

She looked into his eyes, unaware of the heat, the longing that was there for him to see. "Well, I wouldn't have put it that way," she finally said.

He rubbed his jaw, shaking his head. "Should I just put last night up to the adrenaline in your system after the fight?" he asked.

Her eyes widened and she initially thought about denying it, but then she stopped herself just in time. That was a perfect excuse. And maybe it was true.

No, she thought with honesty, it wasn't true. But it would do for an explanation.

"I guess that's probably what it was," she finally said but didn't want to state it as the complete truth. She couldn't outright lie to Xander.

"I'm sorry I took advantage of you last night then," he said as he stepped around her to look out the window. "I wanted to assure you that it won't happen again. I know I was out of line. I took you back to my place to take care of you, to make sure that you were okay and I…" he stopped, sighing. "I'm sorry," he said again.

Turning around, he looked down into her eyes, willing her to tell him that it had nothing to do with the adrenaline. That it had everything to do with wanting him as a man. But those pretty brown eyes couldn't meet his. And he felt like more of an ass than before.

Damn, why couldn't he just leave her alone? Why was he so drawn to this one woman? She didn't feel the same and never had. Now, he'd just compounded their problem by taking advantage of her. He'd acted like a cheap, horrible suit by being all over her last night. Every time she'd moved, he'd been turned on, his mind and control obliterated by the fact that she was finally in his bed, in his arms and kissing him back like she had in so many of his dreams over the past several years.

But even now, being so close to her, smelling her soft shampoo and the strawberry shower gel she used, he wanted to pull her into his arms, sweep everything off of the desk behind her and make love to her until she couldn't speak any longer.

If only he hadn't gotten out of bed this morning. But he'd had to. He'd made love to her so many times last night; all he'd wanted to do was bury himself inside her again. He'd woken up with her soft body wrapped around him, her slender arms holding him close and his body had hardened like a teenage boy on his first date.

Only Autumn had this effect on him. He wanted her so painfully and all she wanted from him was distance.

He had no choice now. He'd had his shot last night. He'd have to back off, give her the space she wanted. He wouldn't even manipulate the office space again when she tried to move off of his floor. Maybe if he didn't see her every day, didn't smell her soft, feminine scent or see her in those sexy, high heels she preferred, he would get over her. And maybe, if she wasn't on his floor, he wouldn't picture her in those lacy nothings he'd picked up last night.

"Well, I just wanted to make sure we were okay," he said, trying to fill that awkward silence once again.

She forced a smile. "Thank you very much for your concern. I'm really okay," she said, looking down, embarrassed by the need she felt when he was this close.

And then he did something completely unexpected. He stepped forward, so close she could just lean forward and they would be touching again, his fingers sliding down her jaw right where the bruise was. His fingers were so light on her skin she could barely feel him. "Does it hurt?" he asked softly.

"No," she said, because in truth, she wasn't feeling anything right now. She couldn't even tell him what day it was or if the sun was out. Her whole world was focused on this one man and his gentle touch. "I thought I'd covered it up well enough."

He smiled slightly, that half smile that made him look sexier than James Bond. "You did. If I hadn't seen it develop last night, I wouldn't know it was there."

She blushed, thinking he'd definitely seen it all last night, including the ugly bruise on her ribs.

"I'll take you down to the police station today so you can make a statement."

She thought about that, about being in his presence more than necessary. She knew it wouldn't be a good idea for her. "I can do that," she told him. "Thank you though."

Xander took the hint and stepped back. "Okay then," he said and turned towards the doorway. "You look beautiful," he finally said before walking out of her office.

Autumn stood there for a long time, her mind going over those words again and again. She'd dressed with him in mind for so long and he'd finally seen her. And now everything was so wrong!

She slumped down into her chair, burying her face in her hands and praying that she wouldn't burst into tears. After several more minutes, she told herself to pull it together. She took a deep breath and lifted herself up. Looking at her computer, she realized that she had over fifty e-mail messages and knew from experience that most of them would be action items. There was nothing slow or plodding about the daily tasks at The Thorpe Group. Everything seemed to happen at warp speed. So no time to feel sorry for the mess she'd just made of her life. She had to get back to work.

She was fine all that day, but had to work hard to avoid Xander. He seemed to be everywhere. She saw him in the copy room, in the office kitchen and even when she was heading to the elevator to leave for lunch. When she saw that, she simply turned around, acting like she was heading for the stairway instead of the elevator. It didn't matter that she had her purse over her shoulder and her coat on her arm. She might look ridiculous walking down the stairs, and it might even be obvious to him that she was avoiding him. But she didn't care. There was no way she was getting into that elevator with Xander. The space was too small, he was too big and her need for him to touch her like he'd done last night was too intense. She'd make a fool of herself and she was tired of doing that.

By the middle of the next day, she was exhausted and hiding out in her office. She slumped down in her chair, idly scrolling through her e-mail messages, trying to find an issue that could be taken care of without her needing to leave the confines of her office.

"What are you going to do about finding me an administrative assistant?" Xander asked, stepping into her office.

Autumn jerked upright, her hungry eyes taking in his tall, handsome frame despite the furious look in his eyes and his hands fisted on his hips.

"Um…" she blinked. She'd been avoiding that issue for the past several days, not sure how to work with him without actually talking to him, seeing him or getting close to him in any way.

"I need someone, Autumn. The last three haven't worked out at all. So the next one has to be pretty exceptional."

She knew that. She'd found fabulous assistants for all three of his brothers, plus all of the other lawyers. She'd just had miserable luck trying to find someone to handle Xander.

"Yes. You're right," she said, digging deep within herself to find the last vestiges of her professionalism. "I'll get right on that. And I'm sorry that…"

His voice was almost gentle but still firm when he interrupted her. "No more sorries, Autumn. Just find me someone who can dig me out of this administrative mess the last one created. I know you have a slew of resumes that you keep on hand of potential candidates. Go through them and bring me the best ones by four o'clock. We'll start the interviews again in two days." With that, he walked out of her office.

She sighed and slumped right back down into her chair, her head dropping into her hands in defeat.

"Are you okay?" Mary asked, walking into Autumn's office.

Autumn grimaced. "I guess so." Her fingers flicked over her keyboard. "Know of any good assistants who are looking for a job?" she asked. Xander was right. She had an archive of support personnel, but he'd already rejected the good ones that she had on file.

Mary shrugged. "I know a couple of people. They aren't legal assistants though."

Autumn could just imagine Xander's reaction to that. "Probably not good," she replied. "I guess I'd better call around to the agencies, see what they can give me."

"I thought that approach was more expensive."

"It is," Autumn explained, mentally irritated that Xander was putting her to that level of effort just because he was so demanding. He'd rejected several, very good candidates because he had such specific needs for his administrative support staff. "But I've got to get someone really good this time. Someone who can fix all the issues that the previous three messed up."

"I can help," Mary said. "Maybe if the two of us worked on the files, we could get things cleaned up."

Autumn thought about that for a moment. She knew she could get the files fixed relatively quickly, but that would mean being close to Xander all day long. She needed to avoid that if possible. "I'll keep that offer in mind. But let me see what I can dig up before we go that route."

Mary disappeared and Autumn picked up the phone. For the next two hours, she called the employment agencies, review resumes and created a chart with the various possibilities and their skills, the pros and cons of each candidate. She also generated a comment sheet to prepare for the interview process, a system she'd developed over the years as a good way to write up notes on a candidate while the ideas and impressions were fresh in the interviewer's mind.

At four o'clock, she nervously brought all her materials into the conference room, set up the copies for Xander and set hers on the other side so she was facing him. In the past, he'd sat down next to her and it had always made her nervous. This way, she could at least have some space and maybe she wouldn't get so angry by his rejections.

Of course, if he rejected candidates without any reason, she'd fight him on the issue. She hated it when he rejected a candidate, simply saying, "I don't like him," or "She struck me wrong." It wasn't fair to the candidates to not have a fair shake at the job simply because they formatted their resume differently than he preferred.

Xander walked into the conference room and saw the stack of resumes placed on the opposite side of the table. He knew exactly what she was doing. For a moment, he thought about letting her get away with it, but in the end, he wasn't that nice of a guy.

He grabbed the papers from across the table and slid them in front of the chair right next to hers, ignoring the look of horror in her eyes. "So who are we going to look at today?" he asked, stretching his legs out so they were close to hers.

For the next two hours, they argued over the candidates' resumes. Back and forth, Autumn pointed out the benefits of one person over another while he chose other candidates that he thought looked better, at least on paper.

"You can't reject someone simply because they 'sound' too young," Autumn snapped at him.

"Yes I can," he countered coolly. "He doesn't have enough experience. Next?"

"Stop! That's ridiculous. What part of your requirements does he not have?" she demanded, sliding the job description towards him.

He actually had the audacity to sit there and point out that the resume didn't spell out a person's organizational skills. "That's a big deal to me after the last person you brought in."

"You agreed that Rosa was a good candidate!" she cried back, defending their joint decision.

"Only after you argued that she would work out. You convinced me. I took your advice. Rosa was nice, but she was an idiot. I need someone who can think."

"You need someone who can follow orders blindly!" she snapped right back. "You don't want a human being," she said, exasperated by all of his demands. "You want a robot."

"Do you have one?" he came right back.

She tossed her arms up in the air, defeated. "So none of these candidates meet your requirements?" she asked, totally dumbfounded.

"Not a single one," he said and leaned forward, ostensibly to look through all the dozen or so resumes she'd brought with her. But in reality, he just wanted to smell her hair, feel her soft skin one more time. He didn't touch her, not getting any signals that she would be receptive to any touch from him. But that didn't mean he couldn't dream.

He stood up, needing to get away from her before he took her into his arms and kissed her senseless. "Have some more resumes for me by tomorrow morning."

Without another word, he walked out of the conference room, leaving her glaring at his back while her eyes shot arrows at his head.

The following morning was exactly the same. By the end of the hour, he'd rejected all of the candidates and Autumn was flabbergasted. "You're being unreasonable!" she yelled at him and then looked at him with a horrified expression.

"I'm sorry!" she gasped. She'd never yelled at anyone before but she was too nervous around him to be able to control her temper. She could smell his cologne and his soap and she ached to just curl up in his lap and feel his strong arms wrap around her, make her feel better.

Xander stared back at her for a long moment, then burst out laughing. "Don't be sorry," he said and put a hand on her back. She flinched away and he pulled back immediately, but he wanted so badly to…well, to do everything to her.

"How about if we go out to lunch today to discuss options?" he suggested, leaning against the conference room table.

Autumn took a deep breath, trying to calm herself down. "Perhaps we should just meet and discuss your requirements again." And maybe get two people in to help him out since no one candidate seemed to meet all of his needs. "We don't need to go out to lunch."

Xander looked down at his watch, shaking his head. "I didn't think it would take this long to get some candidates lined up for interviews. The only time I have available is lunch time."

Autumn sighed, resigned to having lunch with him. "Fine," she said, thinking she could just run down to the deli and grab both of them something so they could eat while they discussed new resumes. Although how she was going to find even more resumes in just a couple of hours she had no clue. Not to mention, her stomach always acted weird around him so eating might be difficult. Maybe if he would finally sit across the table from her instead of next to her!

He walked out of the conference room at that point and she slumped down in the soft, leather chair, feeling defeated. She'd gone through all of her resources to find this second set of resumes. She couldn't figure out where else to go for a new batch. Maybe if she were honest with him, told him that she was stumped, he would relent a bit.

Then she thought about his irritated expression when she'd passed by his office earlier today. Tilly must have been looking for some file and Xander was standing behind her impatiently. Normally, she required her support staff to know exactly where things were, to have files pulled before they were needed. If Xander had a meeting with a client, he'd need the files for that client pulled the night before so he could take them home to review at night if he'd wanted. The fact that Tilly was just pulling a file while Xander stood waiting must mean she wasn't doing an adequate job.

Par for the course, she thought as she gathered up all of the resumes and charts she'd created. Perhaps someone had come into one of the agencies this morning that would be the ideal candidate. And maybe, if all the planets aligned and the stars were shining down on her today, the candidate could come in for an interview this afternoon. Then she'd be free from any further discussions with the man she was growing to hate.

She walked slowly back to her office, wondering where all of his charm had gone. Xander used to be one of those men who could make women go gaga with just his smile. How had he ended up with such horrible employees lately?

Okay, the last one was her fault. But what about the ones before? The previous two had been wonderful. Until the day they'd walked out in fury over Xander's continuous demands. She'd spoken to them as they'd cried out their frustration with their jobs. Nothing they had told her seemed unreasonable. Perhaps she'd been with The Thorpe Group for so long she didn't realize the pressure new people had to endure to get up to speed. Things probably worked faster here. People definitely looked busy non-stop throughout the day.

She passed by Xander's office again on her way back and she cringed when she caught Xander once again leaning against the wall, impatiently waiting for Tilly to find something for him.

She hugged her files closer to her and walked on by, head down and ashamed that she hadn't been able to fix this problem. It had been going on for much too long and Xander was right. He should have someone that can do the job properly. He had too much to worry about and the lack of a good support team was an enormous burden.

Hurrying back to her office, she dumped the rejected resumes and picked up her phone. She would get him the perfect candidate, even if it killed her. Ninety minutes later, she had five more resumes to show Xander. She walked nervously down the hallway with her notebook and pencil, clutching the resumes in her hand.

She hesitated before she knocked though. Looking at him, her heart did something weird inside her chest. He looked so serious as he sat behind his huge desk, reviewing something that looked complicated and important. She stared at his tanned, sexy hands and long fingers that could touch her so gently she went wild. Currently, though, they held a red pen; she wanted to lean over his shoulder and see what he was scribbling in the margins. He had his suit jacket off so she could better see the muscles in his arms and shoulders, muscles she remembered touching so well that her fingertips ached to feel them again.

"Ready to go?" he asked, tossing his pen down onto his desk and standing up.

"Go?" she repeated blankly, still standing in his doorway. "I was just going to run downstairs to the deli and grab a sandwich for us," she replied, her pen hovering over her notebook, ready to take his order so she could escape quickly. "We can just eat our meal in one of the conference rooms."

He shook his head and grabbed his suit jacket, sliding those long, strong arms into the sleeves. "We're getting out of here. A change of scenery is probably going to help."

Autumn was shaking her head even as he walked out of his office, coming closer to her so quickly she had trouble telling her feet to move out of the way. She stood beside his door, awkwardly trying to argue with him, but he just ignored her stammers and spoke directly to his temporary assistant. "Tilly, could you call Mary and have her grab Autumn's coat? We'll meet her in the lobby."

Autumn didn't like this one little bit. She didn't want to leave the office with him. She felt safer here, more secure and able to keep her mind on business. Going out of the office meant dangerous territory. Unknown territory. She didn't like unknown and dangerous. And Xander scared her on so many levels. So much more now than before she'd been in his house and in his bed.

"You really don't…"

"I really do," he countered and put a hand to the small of her back, nudging her out of his area.

The ever efficient Mary was already standing in the lobby with Autumn's coat and purse. Xander handed Mary the notebook and pen Autumn had been holding, then held her coat up for her.

Autumn stared up at him, her stomach clenching at the idea of putting her arms into her coat because then his hands would be on her shoulders. It would almost feel like he was hugging her. Her knees started wobbling at that idea and she took a deep, painful breath. There was nothing to do but put her coat on, and move out of the way as quickly as possible. Her hands dove into the sleeves but the rest was a blur. She felt his hands on her shoulders and froze. Then he did something equally crazy. His fingers moved carefully under her hair, sliding against her neck and sparking more shivers to shoot down her spine.

She had no idea what he was doing. All she knew was that his hands were touching her. She'd dreamed about him doing this again so often over the past few days and now it was happening. His fingers tangled in her hair, running through the tresses. To a casual observer, it probably looked like he was just pulling her hair out from under her coat, but it was so much more than that. It was a caress. A sensual, titillating touch of his fingers that almost knocked her flat.

Their eyes met. She looked over her shoulder at his handsome face and time froze. She could smell his aftershave, feel the heat of his body against her back which had nothing to do with the light wool of her fall coat. She couldn't breathe, couldn't hear anything but the racing of her heart.

And then the sound of the elevator chimed, bringing her back from the fantasy she was having about him turning her around and kissing her. Voices broke through and the almost constantly ringing phones started to come back. She jerked away, taking several steps to put some distance between them. She looked at the floor as her trembling fingers buttoned up her coat.

"Thank you," she whispered, taking her purse from his hands as well.

"My pleasure," he came right back.

Then that hand was back! Right there in the center of her back. She thought that perhaps her entire nervous system started and ended in that exact spot where his hand was resting on her back because every cell in her body tingled, acutely aware of his touch.

"Where are we going?" she asked when they were out of the building and in the October sunshine. It was warmer than expected so she slipped her coat off of her shoulders, turning her face up to the sun.

"Would you rather eat at Antoine's or Durango's?" he asked, watching her as she absorbed the heat on her lovely face. "Or we could just jet off to Aruba so you could get more sunshine," he teased.

Autumn's eyes popped open and she looked up into his amused face. "Sorry," she blushed. "I love October and the cooler temperatures but it's still warm enough to enjoy the outdoors."

"What's your favorite season?" he asked, putting a hand on her back to guide her towards Antoine's, one of the city's most exclusive restaurants.

She realized immediately where they were heading and pulled back. "Would you mind if we went to Durango's instead?"

"Sure. Why?" he asked, but they headed in the opposite direction for the more casual restaurant.

She bit her lip and admitted, "I've just wanted a burger for a long time."

He laughed but they went inside the darker bar and restaurant. The owner immediately recognized them and seated them at one of the windows. "I have five new…"

"We can talk about those later. Let's just relax and have lunch," he suggested. And with that, they talked about everything but work and resumes. During the entire lunch while they downed greasy burgers and cheese topped fries, they talked like they had so long ago, as friends and people instead of combatants.

It was probably the nicest lunch she'd had in years, Autumn thought as she walked back to the office that afternoon.

CHAPTER 4

Autumn glared at the man's back, so angry she couldn't even speak. She'd had fights with Xander before, but this was above and beyond. She couldn't believe he was being this stubborn! Every one of these resumes would be an ideal candidate for his assistant. How could he have rejected all of them? Impossible!

Now she knew he was simply being unreasonable and that infuriated her even more than if he simply disagreed. He'd be wrong in this case. And in many cases, but that was different.

Oh! That man just….infuriated her!

How could he justify being so arbitrary?

Autumn walked back to her office and practically threw her stack of resumes onto her desk, uncaring that several other reports fell off the other side because of the force of her throw.

Mary came in behind her, eyes wide and her body language wary. "I guess your meeting didn't go well?" she asked carefully.

"That's an understatement!" she exclaimed, then tried to calm down by taking several deep breaths.

Mary tried to suppress a smile, but she was glad her boss had her back turned towards her because she didn't think she was very successful. "So your meeting was with Xander, I take it?" she suggested, then took an involuntary step backwards when Autumn spun around, her eyes on fire.

"Sorry, I shouldn't have asked."

Autumn closed her eyes and took several deep breaths. "No, I'm sorry, Mary. I've been acting horribly lately and none of this is your fault. What's worse, I'm taking it out on you and that's not fair." Autumn tried to calm down, but every time she pictured Xander in that conference room demanding more resumes. He wouldn't even talk to some of these candidates and they were the best of the best!

"So what are you going to do next?"

Autumn was stumped. She'd gone to all of her sources three different times. There weren't any other candidates out there! "I have no idea," she said and fell backwards into her chair. "The man really is impossible."

Mary put her hand over her mouth. "I think you said that already."

Autumn chuckled but then glared teasingly at her assistant. "If you're going to point out the obvious, I'm going to assign you as his assistant."

Mary's eyes widened and she backed up, her palms held outwards as if she were being held up at gunpoint. "Not that!" she begged. "Anything but that! Xander Thorpe is a hottie, but he's also mean and irascible. I'd rather not have to deal with him on a daily basis."

Autumn knew exactly what she meant. And it was an odd thing too because Xander hadn't ever been this exacting before. She remembered him at lunch yesterday and she couldn't believe he was the same man. She simply didn't understand what had happened with all of his assistants. Why had they left so quickly and why was it so hard to find someone to take over? She couldn't even promote someone into that position because no one wanted it.

Not that Xander would agree to have anyone already employed, she thought.

"If you have any suggestions, please let me know."

Mary's lips compressed for a long moment before she finally took a breath and suggested, "I think it's time for a shopping trip. You haven't gotten any new shoes in a long time. Why don't you go out and treat yourself."

Autumn's eyes dropped down to her feet and she examined her black shoes. They were still a good pair of shoes, but they could stand to be replaced. The edges were worn away a bit and the heel was starting to wear down.

Besides, shoe shopping really did make her feel much better. It was completely superficial, but she truly felt better when she was wearing a good pair of shoes. A pair that went with her outfit, but even better, a pair of shoes that brought her entire outfit together so it was perfect.

Autumn smiled and stood up. "I think that's a great idea," she said. "And you're right. Shoe shopping really does make me feel better."

"That's the spirit!" she said, clapping her hands together, relieved that her boss was going to go out and get some fresh air. The tension in the office because of the war between these two had become so thick it could be cut with a dull knife. "Go have some fun. And don't come back until you feel better. I'll take care of everything around here."

Autumn grabbed her purse but left her coat. It was a beautiful, sunny day and it had warmed up enough so a coat wasn't necessary. She loved these gorgeous fall afternoons when the sun was shining, the skies were crystal blue and the humidity was so low that her hair didn't go flat. In other words, a perfect shopping day!

"I'll see you a bit later," she said, checking to make sure her phone was on in case an emergency came up and she needed to rush back.

Autumn walked out of the office, feeling better than she had in a long time. There was something about buying a good pair of shoes, or even the anticipation of finding the perfect pair, that made her breathe a little easier, feel much more free.

Xander watched with clenched jaw as Autumn walked out of the office. She had a spring in her step and a smile on her face. Since they'd both been yelling at each other, that could only mean one thing. She was going out with a guy.

He wanted to slam his fist into something and actually had to restrain himself when his brother Ash walked up to him. "Hey, I need your help on something."

Xander turned to face Ash – who took one look at his older brother and stopped, actually taking a step backwards and holding out his hands. "What did I do?" he asked, trying to understand his brother's current mood.

Xander took a breath and shook his head. "Nothing. Sorry. What do you need?" he asked.

"This woman, I think…" and the two of them walked into Xander's office to discuss a legal matter. When they were finished, Ash stood up and pounded his brother on his back. "Was that Autumn heading out, looking so happy?" he asked.

Xander's mood took a dive once again. "What of it?" he demanded.

"Just that she's been looking pretty miserable lately. Any idea what's going on?"

Xander's stomach twisted. If other people were noticing that Autumn was upset, he must have been really tough on her. He rubbed his forehead, wishing he could do something to clear the air between the two of them. It was a constant battle to keep his hands off of her. But the only way he knew to keep her talking to him was to reject all of her candidates. He was being an ass though. He had to relent.

He picked up the stack of resumes one more time and looked through the candidates. "She's trying to find me a new assistant," Xander explained.

Ash nodded his head, but he didn't really understand. "So you pissed her off?"

Xander pulled three resumes out of the stack of twenty that he and Autumn had reviewed in the past two days. "Yes. I've been pretty annoying." And then he thought of her bright, shining face when she'd left a moment ago and he felt that gut-punch again.

"So she must be off shoe shopping again, eh?"

Xander's eyes snapped up to his youngest brother's, confusion in his eyes. "Shoe shopping?" he repeated.

Ash shrugged. "Sure. Anytime she's really upset, or you've just annoyed her to the point where she's reached the limit of her patience, she goes shoe shopping.

By the time she gets back to the office, everything is all better and she's smiling again." Ash punched Xander on the arm as he walked quickly out the door. "At least until she has to deal with you again, that is."

Xander stood there in the middle of his office, almost light-headed from the relief he was feeling. Ash was right. That smile and the hop in her step were more likely due to her going out and hitting the shops. It probably didn't have anything to do with her having a date with anyone!

He threw back his head and laughed, feeling awesome all of a sudden.

But when his relief was finished, he was still grinning, but he also knew he'd have to make things right again. He'd been pretty horrible to her this morning. And most likely, very unreasonable.

Grabbing his suit coat, he walked quickly out of his office. "I'll be back in a while, Tilly," he said to the woman who jerked in fright now every time he spoke to her. He might have some areas to patch up with her as well. She wasn't the brightest bulb in the package, but she wasn't as bad as how he'd been treating her. Or maybe she was just nervous because he was always arguing with Autumn, her boss while she was working here.

Once he was out on the street, he walked quickly, his eyes scanning the people walking on the sidewalk and looking into the various stores, trying to find Autumn. He caught her just as she was walking into the big department store on the next block. He picked up his pace and caught up with her as she was entering the shoe department.

He watched with a mixture of amusement and interest as she walked by several shoes, picking them up, examining one, flexing another, sticking her finger inside and doing something. A salesperson approached her and she looked longingly at two different pairs of shoes, one black and one red. But she walked over to the discount shoe rack and picked up a pair of sexy, black heels. They weren't as hot as the ones she had looked at a moment ago, but they were nice enough. He stayed in the background, but worked his way over to the sales desk, ensuring that he kept out of her line of sight. When the sales clerk was coming back with the shoes she'd selected in her size, Xander pulled him over. "Bring her the shoes in her size she'd been looking at several minutes ago, okay?" he asked.

The salesperson looked him up and down, then smiled, acknowledging the hand-tailored suit and Indian cotton shirts. Salespeople the world over knew how to pick up the signals of a wealthy customer and cater to them. This one was no exception.

He quickly delivered the originally requested shoes, but then went back to get the other pairs in Autumn's size. While Xander waited, he picked up several other shoes that he thought she might like, plus a few others that he personally liked.

Handing all of them to the salesclerk, he piled the man high with the shoes, telling him to bring all of them in her size as well.

Then Xander sat down in one of the chairs and watched as Autumn tried on each pair of shoes. He could tell by the expression on her face which ones she liked and which she didn't like. The salesperson was perfect, telling her that he didn't have anything else to do so he didn't mind getting her shoes in the various sizes "just for fun" was what he said.

Each time Autumn tried on a new pair, if she liked it, Xander would signal to the salesperson to put them in one pile. If she didn't like the shoe, the clerk put them in another pile. It was the best lunchtime break he'd had in a long, long time. Well, besides the lunch he'd spent with her at Durango's yesterday. She'd been so fun and free, talking about everything and anything. He'd enjoyed just looking at her smiling face.

In the end, she purchased her discounted, black shoes and walked out of the store, still feeling pretty good. When she was out of sight, Xander walked up to the salesclerk and handed him his credit card. Put all the others in the 'like' pile on this credit card and have them sent to this address," he told the man who looked like he had just about won the lottery today due to the commission he'd earn on this shoe extravaganza.

On the way out, he picked up a box of pretty chocolates, thinking they might go a ways towards soothing Tilly's panic every time he asked her for something. As the cashier was ringing up that purchase, he saw another box of chocolates. This one was bigger, more elaborate and he immediately thought of Autumn. "Can you wrap that box up," he said to the cashier. "Have them sent to this address?" he told her, handing him another business card. On the back, he wrote Autumn's name and her extension, just in case.

"Thanks," and he smiled, walking out of the store with the smaller box of chocolates, feeling much better. Autumn loved shoes, but she was a huge fan of chocolates too.

Back in her office, Autumn pulled her old shoes off and slid her feet into the new ones, loving the way the supple leather enclosed her foot. She stood up and walked around her office, making sure that they still felt good while she was on the carpeting. Smiling, she walked down the hallway, a definite perk in her step. She wasn't even going to tackle the problem of trying to find new candidates for Xander today. She felt too good and she didn't want to spoil the mood. She'd figure something out tomorrow, she told herself as she slowly whittled down her workload that had been piling up over the past few days since she'd spent so much time trying to find Xander a new assistant.

She sighed as the tension left her body with each step and felt wonderful. She stayed on the opposite end of the hallway from Xander, not wanting to ruin this good mood by running into him and having him demand more resumes. Resumes which she didn't have right now, since she was purposely ignoring his problem.

When she came back to her office an hour later, she noticed a strange look on Mary's face. "What's up?" Autumn asked, her hand resting on the doorknob to her office. "And why is my office door closed?"

Mary smiled weakly, then shrugged. "I didn't know what to do with all of them, so I just stacked them in your office," she explained.

"Stacked what up?" Autumn asked, confused.

"All the boxes."

Autumn still didn't understand. "Did an order come in that didn't fit in the storage room?" she asked, pushing open the door. And then she just stopped.

Her office wasn't filled, but there were definitely a lot of boxes on her desk. Bags with about ten different boxes. Shoe boxes! And a huge box of chocolates sat on the corner of her desk.

"What's all this?" Autumn asked, wondering what kind of mistake had been made. "Where did all of these come from?"

She opened one box and saw the red, suede shoes she'd absolutely loved earlier this afternoon. "Oh my!" she gasped. Opening the next one, she saw the black ones with the zipper on the size. Box after box revealed all the beautiful shoes that she'd tried on earlier. "I didn't buy these," she whispered, her voice completely gone as her heart beat frantically. "At least, I don't think I did," she said. She pulled her receipt out of the smaller bag and looked. Sure enough, there was only one pair of shoes on that receipt.

"There's definitely been a mistake," she said. "Some of these shoes are way out of my price range. I can't spend this much money on shoes!"

Mary was sighing as she held up a pair of lime green, leather shoes with a gold bow on the side. "Can you keep them for a day or two? I just like holding them," she said with awe in her eyes.

Autumn didn't even answer her, too busy looking up the phone number of the department store. It took her several tries, but she eventually was connected to the shoe department. And miracle of miracles, the salesclerk who had helped her earlier was actually still there.

"Hi there," she said with as friendly a tone of voice as she could. "I was there earlier today and you helped me try on several pairs of shoes."

"Yes ma'am," the clerk replied with a friendly, deferential tone. "Did you receive the delivery?" he asked politely.

"Um," Autumn stared around at all the boxes of shoes. "Well, yes. I got more than ten pairs of shoes, but there's been some mistake. I didn't buy all of these," she explained. "I need to return them."

"No mistake ma'am. You won a sort of lottery this afternoon. All those shoes are bought and paid for. I hope you enjoy them!" he said with enthusiasm running through his voice.

She didn't say anything for a long moment. "Are you sure?" she asked.

"Absolutely. Please come back and visit us soon! And let me know if I can be of any future assistance."

Autumn thanked the man before she hung up, her eyes still staring at all the shoes around her office. Mary had pulled out several more shoes, trying on all of them in the vain hope that they might be a different size, several sizes larger, so she could steal one or two of them. No such luck, she accepted when the last of the boxes of shoes was opened.

"What did the guy say?" Mary asked, running her finger down the side of a black, patent leather shoe with a gold tipped heel that almost looked lethal.

Autumn picked up a grey flannel pair. She'd thought they were like slippers but they had a slightly higher heel. "He said I won the afternoon shopping lottery." She'd loved these so much but they were way too expensive. Oh, she knew that some people spent two or three thousand dollars on one pair of shoes and these were only in the two or three hundred dollar range, but still! Her price range was more along the lines of fifty to one hundred dollars, a bit more when it was a high quality pair or something she simply had to have.

And she'd never bought this many pairs of shoes at one time!

Something just didn't sound right about the whole thing. Windfalls like this simply didn't happen to her. She'd never won anything in her life.

"I wish I'd gone with you," Mary said and put the last pair of shoes back in the box, carefully pushing the tissue back in place. "Well, better get back to work. Since no shoe fairy is going to hand me twelve pairs of shoes, I need to earn more money so I can buy my own."

Mary laughed at her silly joke as she walked back out to her desk.

Autumn stacked the boxes of shoes back up, pushing them into the bags while her mind whirled through the possibilities. The shoe lottery didn't make any sense!

Then she looked at her desk and spotted the box of chocolates. Chocolates? She never got chocolates because she ate them all! She couldn't have chocolates around or she'd gain ten pounds!

Ignoring the chocolates, she continued to work, even pulled up a few more resumes but rejected them since they didn't look better than the ones she'd already discussed with Xander. She didn't realize the passing of time, but by the time she looked up, it was past eight o'clock at night.

Autumn leaned back in her chair and stared at the stack of shoes. If it didn't make sense, she couldn't accept it. Maybe if she spoke to the store manager tomorrow, she would feel a little better about the windfall. But right now, she didn't understand it, so she didn't get excited about all the shoes.

"Autumn I was wondering…" Ash stood in the doorway, his eyes frozen as he took in the stack of shoes in their bags. "Man he must have really pissed you off," Ash said as he counted the number of shoe boxes. "Twelve pairs of shoes?" he exclaimed. "What did that ass do to you that you needed to buy twelve pairs?" he asked, becoming angry on her behalf.

Autumn was completely confused. "What are you talking about and who made me angry?"

Ash shrugged. "Xander of course. He's pretty much the only one you fight with. Did he do this to you?" Ash demanded.

Her mind worked quickly through his comments, trying to interpret what he was saying. "Did Xander make me so angry that I bought twelve pairs of shoes? Is that what you're asking me?"

Ash shook his head. "I'll talk to him Autumn. I know that something is wrong, but I promise, I'll get him to apologize." He glanced at the stack of shoes once more.

"What are you talking about?" she demanded, standing up and looked up at him. "How is Xander involved in the shoe issue?"

Ash looked at her, then at the shoes. "This afternoon, when you were leaving I could tell that you were in a better mood."

"And?" she prompted when he didn't go on.

"And," he laughed, "Xander was right next to me and I mentioned you looked happy because you were going shoe shopping."

Autumn simply stared at him, trying to connect the dots.

Ash was starting to look uncomfortable. "Isn't that what you do when he pisses you off?" he asked, obviously still confused by the intricacies of the female mind.

"He's been…" she searched her mind for an appropriate word, careful since Ash was Xander's younger brother. They were the closest siblings she'd ever met so she didn't want to insult anyone.

"Xander's been an ass, Autumn. I don't know what's going on, but I'll talk with him."

Ash turned and walked out of her office, forgetting whatever it was he was going to ask of her. She looked at the stack of shoes, her mind whirling with the possibilities. She pulled out a black and white polka dotted pair, her finger smoothing over the fabulous material.

And then it hit her. She hadn't won any ridiculous lottery! Somehow, Xander had paid for these shoes!

She grabbed the polka dotted shoes and stormed out of her office, straight down the hallway. Everyone else was pretty much gone for the night but she saw the light in his office and was thrilled that her prey was still available.

"You bastard!" she called out, completely ignoring all office protocols as her anger took over. She wasn't thinking, just reacting to the fact that Xander had bought her all of these shoes as a way to placate her!

Xander had been sitting behind his desk, the papers he was working on illuminated by just his desk light so when he looked up to watch her storm into his office, she couldn't see his face very well. She didn't care. Not one little bit. He'd tried to buy her! "You're a horrible, evil, ridiculous scoundrel!" she said and threw the shoe across the room at him.

Xander was never so glad that he'd played football in high school and college. And that his instincts hadn't diminished over time. His boxing workouts probably helped here as well. He was easily able to duck the flying shoe-missile. When he looked up again, he saw that she had another shoe primed and ready to fire and he went into survival mode, his face breaking out in a huge grin as he took on the challenge of a furious Autumn. Damn, she looked hot in her new shoes!

He rounded his desk, his hands open in a placating gesture. "Autumn, I have no idea what you're thinking, but let's talk about this," he said. No sooner had the words left his mouth that he had to duck when she threw the second shoe right at his head. Thankfully, he was pretty good at dodging fists in the ring, which lent itself well to dodging shoes.

"You bought all these shoes, didn't you?"

Xander realized he was caught but he was too busy trying to figure out how to avoid getting bashed in the head to come up with a good lie. She was so angry, she reached down and whipped off the shoe she was wearing, firing it just as hard.

Xander knew he had to hurry up and tackle her before he was impaled on those shoes. And he also had to stop thinking she looked incredibly sexy when she was threatening him with bodily harm.

"Let's talk, Autumn."

"NO! We've been talking for the last three days and all you do is drive me crazy! I'm done talking with you. And just when I have things worked out in my mind, you go out and buy me shoes! How crazy is that?" And there flew the last shoe.

He didn't take any chances. Going in low, before she could grab the books on the bookshelf, he dove for her middle. With both grace and gentleness, he plowed into her and pinned her back against the wall. She struggled for all she was worth but he wasn't letting up. His hands held her arms above her head and his body pinned the rest of her. He just watched, fascinated while she struggled, writhing against him. In the end, his pinning her didn't stop her. It was her realization that she was turning him on that froze her movements.

When she was finally still but out of breath, he smiled down at her. "So how about you tell me why you are so angry with me," he said, but his mind was on the way her breasts were now flattened against his chest. He didn't really give a damn about her anger. Well, he did, but that was for later. After he…

Autumn groaned when he bent low and nibbled on her earlobe.

"Tell me what I did wrong," he said, sincerely confused.

Autumn looked up at him, her body on pins and needles, wishing he would kiss her, make love to her just like he had that one night. And then she remembered all the other women in his life and she burst into tears.

All sexual need dissipated with Autumn's first tears. He loved her anger and her passion, thought she was sexy as all get out when she was on a mission to fix something in the office. But tears unmanned him. He couldn't handle tears, not from her! Which was ironic since women had used tears on him all the time and he was always completely unmoved. But when she looked up at him with those sparkling tears in her eyes, he felt like the biggest jerk in the world.

"Autumn, talk to me. How can I fix this?" he asked her gently, holding her close to him as he hugged her against him. When she sagged against his chest, the tears came stronger. He lifted her into his arms and carried her over to his sofa, sitting down with her in his lap, rocking her gently while she cried out her sorrow. He couldn't believe he'd done this to her and he felt worse the longer her tears lasted.

When the tears finally subsided, he pulled back and looked down at her, his arms still around her waist. "Can you talk to me?" he asked gently. "I still don't understand what I did wrong. I thought you loved new shoes."

She sniffed, lifting her face out of his neck, almost bursting into tears again when she saw her makeup smeared against his collar. He probably paid a couple hundred dollars for those shirts of his and she'd just gone and stained one of them. "I'm sorry," she whispered, embarrassed by her outburst. He handed her a tissue and she used it to try and wipe away the mess on his collar.

"That's for you, Autumn," he said and tried to stop her from cleaning his collar.

"But I messed up your shirt."

"Don't worry about that. Tell me what I did wrong."

She sniffed once again and looked away from the mess on his shirt, trying to get off of his lap.

"You're not leaving until you help me understand," he said, his hands tightening around her waist.

She laughed slightly, but it sounded more like a hiccup. "You bought me the shoes, didn't you?" she asked, but she could already see the answer in his eyes.

"What difference does it make if I bought you the shoes or not?"

She took a deep breath, trying to calm down. "It matters because of why you did it. And the cost of all those shoes."

"The cost is nothing," he said, dismissing the expense with a wave of his hand. "Why do you think I bought them for you?"

"Because you made me angry."

"Yes. That's part of it," he said.

She slipped off his lap, needing to put some space between them now that her emotional outburst was finished. "You shouldn't have done that," she said, feeling sad both because he'd bought her shoes to appease his guilt and because she knew she'd have to take back all of those lovely shoes. She shouldn't have, but she'd fallen in love with some of those shoes this afternoon. Just looking at them in their boxes had been a painful temptation. She already had outfits picked out for some of them. "I know you were just trying to make me feel better. And appease your guilt. But I'm okay."

Xander stood up as well, towering over her as only Xander could. Ryker and Axel were about the same height as him and Ash was even taller, but those men didn't seem to do it the same way Xander did. He didn't just stand there. He loomed. He intimidated. He....turned her on when he stood there looking so powerful and dominating. Some people needed oysters or asparagus. Autumn only needed Xander. He was a sexy and enticing aphrodisiac all by himself.

He bent down and picked up one of her shoes, then lifted her up unexpectedly, setting her back onto his desk. "I can't really say that I bought you these shoes to appease my guilt. Although I do apologize for being such an obnoxious, irritating person lately."

She swallowed, barely hearing his words because his fingers were holding her leg, his hand smoothing down the skin of her calf. It was almost as if she weren't wearing stockings at all. When his hand lifted her foot while his other hand put her shoe back on, he said, "What about if you just accept that I like seeing you in these shoes? I like it when you walk down the hallway and you have these sexy heels on, you're sexy skirts and you're sexy makeup, looking like some sort of goddess of business or something."

She couldn't help it. The laugh just sort of escaped. "Goddess of business?" she repeated.

He nodded his head, his hand sliding back up her leg, sneaking under her skirt sensuously. "A goddess anyway." He chuckled as well. "Maybe of more than just business."

She smiled, feeling pretty sexy at that moment. "I really don't want to be a goddess of business," she laughed. She realized where this was going, what her head was thinking and she pulled back. Taking her foot out of his hand, she shook her head. "I'd better get home," she told him and slipped off his desk. "It's been a pretty long and horrible day. I have a feeling Tilly is about to quit on you too."

Xander leaned back against his desk, watching with appreciation as she bent down low to pick up her other shoe and slip it onto her foot. "Don't worry about Tilly," he said as she bent to pick up the other two missiles she'd fired at his head earlier tonight. "I bought her a box of chocolates as an apology."

Autumn was crushed. The shoes and the chocolates. He had a lot to apologize for, she thought warily. "Well, I'd better get out of here."

She turned around and walked to his door. But she stopped and turned around. "I'm sorry for throwing my shoes at you," she said.

Xander laughed softly. "Please feel free to throw any clothing you'd like to take off," he said. Then he got to enjoy the blush that burst into her cheeks before she turned away again and walked down the hallway.

CHAPTER 5

Ash watched Autumn walk down the hallway and he instantly knew something was wrong. He watched her face, noted the dark circles under her eyes and his eyes narrowed. And then it hit him. When he realized what was wrong, his temper almost exploded.

Storming down the hallway, he didn't even bother to knock before he walked into Xander's office. He did hesitate, ensuring that his brother wasn't with a client before he demanded. "What did you do to her?"

Xander turned around, sliding the book back onto the bookshelf that he'd been reading. "Do to who?" he asked, not sure what his brother was talking about. He was exhausted from lack of sleep, frustrated because he couldn't figure out how to get Autumn back into his bed and everything he did seemed to backfire on him. So he definitely wasn't in the mood to deal with his youngest brother right at the moment.

"Autumn!" Ash growled, his hands fisted at his sides.

Xander's eyes narrowed. "What do you mean? What's wrong with her?" he demanded, his body ready to head down the hallway to make sure she was okay.

"That's what I'm asking you!" Ash countered, taking a step forward. "What did you do to her? How did you upset her this time?"

"Why do you think she's upset?"

Ash didn't have time to answer before Axel burst into Xander's office, pushing Ash out of the way in order to confront Xander. "What did you do to her?"

Xander looked from one to the other of his younger brothers, completely befuddled. "What the hell are you two talking about?" He was starting to get angry himself now. He didn't like the idea of Autumn being upset, but more to the point, he didn't like anyone else caring as much about his woman being upset.

"Autumn!" Axel almost yelled. "She's upset about something and you have to be the reason. You've been driving her crazy with all your ridiculous demands and now you've broken her!"

Xander's heart just about stopped with those words. "Tell me what you know!" he growled.

Again, no one could answer because Ryker walked in at that moment. He wasn't as abrasive as his two youngest brothers, but the concern was written all over his features. "Xander, do you know anything about why Autumn is so upset?" he asked, his eyebrows drawn low over his eyes, a strong indicator of how upset he really was. Ryker didn't yell. One had to look into his eyes to know what was going on. He held everything very controlled and close to himself.

Xander threw up his hands with exasperation. "What are you guys all talking about? I spoke to her last night and she was perfectly fine!" Well, at the end she was fine, he thought silently. He wouldn't tell them about her crying. That was between the two of them and he wasn't about to discuss it with his nosy brothers.

"She's obviously upset about something," Ryker said, stepping to the side.

Xander glared at the wall of brothers, wishing, not for the first time, that he'd had only sisters. "If someone doesn't explain this to me, we're going to experience a whole lot more than just words and accusations!" he threatened to all three of them in general. It might be three against one, but he was protecting his woman now and that made him stronger.

"She's wearing flats!" Ash spat out as if shoes without heels were illegal and offensive.

Xander looked at the other two, both of which were nodding their heads in agreement. "She's wearing flats?" he asked, not sure what they meant.

"Yes!" Axel yelled. "So what did you do to her?"

Xander was worried now. What they were saying didn't make any sense at all. "Get out of my way," he growled, trying to push past the three of them.

Axel crossed his arms over his huge chest, glaring intently at his brother. "You're not going near her if you're going to hurt her feelings again."

"And you've got to figure out how to fix this!" Ash told him.

Ryker was in the process of nodding while Xander was considering which one to punch out first. He was frantic to get to Autumn and find out what they were talking about. But a moment before he was going to take a swing, a soft, feminine voice interrupted and broke through his haze of fury.

"What's going on in here?" Autumn asked, stepping around Ryker, Ash and Axel. She looked up at Xander, trying to get an answer. But she felt the blush stain her cheeks when all four men looked down at her feet.

Xander was the first to recover. He looked at her shoes, saw the cheetah print flats that went perfectly with her chocolate brown pants and burst out laughing.

Autumn smiled at his amusement, shaking her head as she looked up at the other three Thorpe brothers.

"Can anyone explain this to me?" she asked while Xander leaned over his desk, bracing himself as his laughter took over his common sense and manners.

Ryker stepped forward and touched her forearm gently. "Are you okay?" he asked, his eyes concerned.

Autumn looked at Xander, still laughing and rolled her eyes. "I had a hard day yesterday, but by the end of it, things were back into perspective."

Ash and Axel relaxed somewhat, but they still looked like they wouldn't mind punching their brother.

"Six o'clock at the gym," Ash told Xander, smacking him on the back before leaving.

"I'll be there too," Axel said and walked out, not bothering to even acknowledge his older brother.

Ryker shook his head, glanced down at Autumn's flat shoes once more, then walked out. "I'll be there too," he told Xander.

Autumn watched three of her four bosses walk out of Xander's office, not sure what was going on. "Would you mind telling me what just happened here?" she asked, speaking over the still-laughing Xander.

When he continued to laugh, she huffed and started to walk out of his office, determined to get things done instead of stand here awkwardly. But he stopped her by grabbing her wrist and pulling her back. He was still laughing, but at least he was somewhat in control now.

She took a deep breath and waited, feeling tiny and silly in her flats, especially next to Xander. He was so darn tall!

"Why are you wearing flats?" he asked, still chuckling. "Is it because of our conversation last night?"

She shifted uncomfortably. "Yes. I didn't want you to think I was trying to lure you into my web."

He lifted a hand to touch her cheek in a feather-like caress. "And what if I want to be lured into your web?"

Her mouth fell open and her body softened. She glanced down at his mouth, then back to his eyes. "You can't do this here," she whispered.

"Where can I do it?"

She was just about to respond when Tilly interrupted them. "Mr. Thorpe, your…" she stopped when she saw the way the two of them were standing. "Oh, I'm sorry," she gasped and tried to back out of the office. "I didn't mean to interrupt."

Autumn looked behind her and pulled out of Xander's grip. "You're not interrupting anything," she said and quickly walked out of Xander's office. She didn't bother to look back at him, cursing herself for falling under that famous spell of his. She couldn't believe how close she'd been to telling him to come over to her house and fall into her web. Thank goodness for Tilly's interruption. She'd been about to make a complete fool of herself.

The next few days, she worked harder than normal. She stayed late so she wouldn't run into Xander leaving with any of his latest lady loves and she came in early. The thought of running into him on the way into the office, perhaps seeing him with a grin on his face which she would automatically think was because he "got lucky" the previous night, would hurt too much to bear. So she assiduously avoided seeing the man, even in the hallways. She knew his routine and worked hard to avoid him.

She was successful until their normal Friday morning staff meeting. Her luck wore out but she was braced for it. The other three Thorpe brothers came in and took their seats but Xander rushed in right before the meeting was to start. Unfortunately, that meant he was sitting right next to her. On the up side, it allowed her to avoid looking at him. Even when he spoke, she could pretend to be writing something. On the down side, she thought she could actually feel the heat of his body even from one chair away. That was impossible, she told herself, feeling ridiculous for even thinking it. But she wasn't aware of her body moving towards that source of incredible heat. Her legs crossed and uncrossed until half of her body was practically facing his.

When the meeting finally adjourned, Autumn looked around, surprised that everyone was getting up and moving out the door. Had she missed the entire meeting? She looked down at her note pad, wondering what she'd written. But the page was basically blank. There were a few doodles, but she'd written nothing else.

Normally, these meetings caused her to take several pages of notes, but not today.

"I'll be there in just a moment," she heard Xander say and her whole body froze.

And then she heard what she'd been dreading she might hear. The door closed.

Slowly, as if her neck muscles were refusing to cooperate, she lifted her head, looking up at Xander as he stood leaning against the door.

"What's going on?" he demanded as he crossed his arms over his massive chest.

Her heart was beating so loudly, she was afraid he might be able to hear it from across the room. "I don't know what you mean," she replied and stood up, straightening all of the papers that had been handed out during the meeting. Some had actually been her handouts. How had they been distributed? She didn't remember any of it.

"Something is obviously wrong," he said and moved so he was standing over her with the back of her thighs pressing against the edge of the conference room table.

She couldn't look at him in the eye so she stared at his chest, afraid of what he might see. And afraid of what she might see in his eyes as well. "I don't know what you mean, Xander. Everything is perfectly fine. Nothing at all is wrong," she stammered nervously. She was lying through her teeth and he probably knew it, but she was going to brave through it as long as possible. The alternative, being honest with Xander, wasn't a possibility.

"Then why did you tell the others that we needed an office change?" he asked softly, his indigo blue eyes looking at her features slowly, as if he were savoring the moment alone with her.

She pulled back slightly, her brain not functioning properly with him so close to her. They always kept their distance especially when they were fighting each other. Except for that…well, that one afternoon.

She hadn't remembered saying anything about an office change so this was all news to her. She'd thought it, especially this week while trying to avoid running into Xander in the hallways.

Trying to keep herself from looking like a complete idiot, she ran with the question as best she could. "What's wrong with an office change?" she whispered, her soft, brown eyes dropping down to look at his mouth. She didn't know that her body language had softened and she was instinctively turning towards him, her fingers fluttering by her side because she wanted to reach out and touch him so badly. She wondered what it would be like to be able to touch him whenever she wanted, to stretch up onto her tip toes and kiss him, to ask him to take her into his arms and make love to her.

She sighed and bowed her head slightly, knowing she didn't have those rights and never would. Xander was every lady's man, not just hers.

Xander's entire body reacted to the way she was looking at him. She was always so standoffish, yelling at him whenever he pressed her buttons. Granted, he pressed them as often as he could, loving the way her face turned all soft pink and flushed when she got angry. But she hadn't snapped at him once today, hadn't risen to any of his verbal jibes during the staff meeting, and she'd even agreed with him on a few issues he'd brought up.

"Nothing is wrong with an office change, Autumn," he said, moving slightly closer to her, filling his nostrils with that pretty, feminine scent he remembered from their one time together. Damn, she smelled so good! And she tasted….

Nope, not thinking of that, he told himself firmly. That boat has already sailed. She didn't want him that way anymore or she wouldn't have run out of his place while he showered. She'd spoken loud and clear that morning.

But what was she telling him now? She wasn't moving away from him, he realized.

"Change is good," she said, barely a whisper this time. She didn't have the strength to raise her voice above a whisper. Not when Xander was this close. Not when she could feel every particle of heat he was emanating from his incredible body. And she was so cold. She'd been so cold for so very long. It wasn't right that he had all this heat and she had...none. It felt like her entire body was aching, desperate for Xander's heat, for him to wrap his arms around her and...yes, to do what he'd done with her that one afternoon.

"We can't be like this," she said, trying to move backwards, willing herself to give up this sudden fascination with...all of him.

"We're in a conference room, discussing business," he replied, but he shifted his body so no one could see them if the door were to open accidentally.

Autumn sighed with relief when he said that. She looked up and around, realizing that her vision was obstructed by his extremely large chest. Had he actually moved closer? Was he bending his head and...oh please don't let him kiss her! Oh please don't let him stop if that was what he planned!

She lifted her head at the same moment his mouth captured hers, wrapping her arms around his neck and pulling him closer. When he deepened the kiss, she opened her mouth, reveling in the hot waves that washed over her as he put his hands on her waist and lifted her up against him.

The force of that kiss made her mind whirl with need and desire. She'd never kissed a man and felt like this before. She couldn't get enough of him, rising up on her tip toes so she could feel more of him against her body, press herself closer and know that, for this instant, this moment in time, he was all hers. She had the freedom and the right to touch him and her fingers moved over his neck, his shoulders then back up to tangle in his hair.

Xander couldn't believe how incredible she felt in his arms. She was all softness and light, heat and energy. He hadn't imagined how it felt to hold her, to feel that incredible power surge through him, making him feel even more powerful simply because she was letting him hold her.

Suddenly, there was a noise outside of the conference room and Autumn broke away. She quickly put several feet between their bodies, just in time actually since a second later, several people opened up the conference room door and were piling in for their scheduled meeting, coming to an abrupt stop when they saw who was already in the room.

Autumn glanced at Xander, then at the group of lawyers who were standing there, mouths open as they tried to figure out what was going on and if they should just back out. Thankfully, Xander's eyes looked furious which was too normal of an occurrence, especially when she was around. The fights between the two of them were becoming legendary around the office.

She quickly gathered up her papers and walked out of the conference room, pretending like nothing unusual had just occurred, that the tension the newcomers felt was simply the normal anger that blew up whenever she and Xander were in a room for more than thirty seconds.

It probably didn't help that her face was red or that she couldn't regain control of her breathing. Her fingers were shaking and her knees not very steady, but they couldn't see that. And if they did, hopefully they would simply attribute those symptoms to a fight as well.

She made her way through the hallways, ignoring anyone who tried to call to her for a question or to let her know whatever it was that they felt she needed to know. She didn't stop until she was in her office alone with the door slammed shut, blocking out the rest of the world and all the craziness that had occurred since she'd been in Xander's arms. She closed her eyes and took several deep breaths, trying very hard to regain her semblance of normalcy.

Had she really just kissed Xander? In a conference room?! Where anyone could, and did, interrupt them! She shook her head and practically fell into her chair, her whole body shaking from the impact of him. Well, actually, she was shaking from her reaction to him and not the man himself.

Okay, so it was most likely a combination of both the man and the way he touched her and the way she reacted to him.

Stop! She closed her eyes and leaned back in her chair.

"Are you okay?" a female voice asked.

Autumn's eyes popped open and she looked back up at her assistant. "Yes. I'm fine," she said and sat forward, placing her hands over her keyboard. She tried to look as if she were working but knew she was failing miserably. It was probably the guilty look in her eyes that gave her away so she looked down at her keyboard. "Why do you ask?"

Mary looked at her curiously. "You rushed in here like the hounds of hell were chasing after you. I guess you've been acting a bit strangely this week so I shouldn't think anything of it, but it just feels like something more is going on." She hesitated for a moment, looking curiously at her boss from the doorway. "And your cheeks are all pink, like you might have a fever or something." Mary walked over to Autumn's desk and handed her a sheaf of papers. "Are you not feeling well? Maybe you're coming down with something. This crazy fall weather, cold in the morning, hot in the afternoon, can do that to a person's system. Our bodies don't know whether to produce heat or find air conditioning. Do you need to go home? I can cover for you. It's Friday so most people are already heading out."

Autumn thought longingly of her home and the solace it would provide. Her comfortable townhouse was exactly what she needed right now. She could skip out of here and hide her head under a pillow, pretend like she never had to come out again.

But what would Xander say if he found out she'd left early. He'd probably show up at her door, just to make sure she was okay. He'd been fairly protective of her lately.

Well one day did not make a protector, she corrected herself. She smiled back to the memory of the three other Thorpe brothers confronting Xander when she'd worn her flat shoes. That made her feel good, all of them ganging up on him to make sure she was okay. She almost chuckled at the confused expression in his eyes, and all because she'd worn a pair of flats. Boy, she'd really thrown everyone off that day!

She shook her head, banishing the memory and all those warm fuzzy feelings Xander tended to generate inside of her whenever he did the he-man-my-woman routine for her benefit. He was probably like that with all the women. He definitely did it to all of his female clients, making sure they were financially protected when their husbands finalized a divorce. She actually liked that about him. Unless he was doing it to the women he dated. She wouldn't like that at all.

Mary was still waiting for a response and she focused on the work she had to get done today. "I'm fine," she smiled wearily. "Just tired. It's been a hectic week."

Mary smiled back and handed her the other reports Autumn had asked for earlier. "The client system is up and running now. All the cases are fully loaded from prior years and can be cross-referenced for any issue or keyword. Several people have already stopped by my desk to compliment you on fighting for that system," Mary commented as she walked out of Autumn's office.

Autumn smiled, feeling a huge sense of victory wash over her with those words. She'd fought hard for that system, arguing with Xander mostly. He'd said they hadn't needed something like that because there were already research databases that were online and the firm subscribed to them. What was the point, he'd asked over and over again. She'd given him several arguments, fighting with him about productivity, the statistics she'd gathered about the various resources, the capability of the support staff to gather data and market more effectively for new clients. The Thorpe Group didn't need more clients, he'd argued. They were turning clients away all the time because they couldn't hire and train new lawyers fast enough.

She'd fought him tooth and nail on every last penny spent on the system so it was a huge relief that it had been easy to implement and that staff members were actually using it. A point for her, she thought.

But somehow, the idea of scoring one more point in their ongoing office battle just didn't make her feel as victorious as it used to. Another problem with sleeping with the enemy, she berated herself one more time. Even winning a point didn't excite her as much.

She sighed and looked around at her office. She'd spent so much time here lately; the space was starting to feel a bit closed in. More like a prison than a sanctuary. Maybe she should head out after all. She wasn't doing much here anyway. Why log the hours when she wasn't being productive? She suspected that, if she left the office for a little while, she might get more done at home. It was worth a try anyway. At least it would get her away from Xander. She simply couldn't run into him again after that kiss! She had no idea how to explain her reaction, or even why she'd let it happen.

She stuffed her bag with work she might do over the weekend, then shut down her laptop and stuffed that into her bag as well.

"Mary, I've changed my mind. I'm going to head out. If anyone asks, just tell them I'm fine but working from home this afternoon."

"Sure thing," Mary replied, barely pausing in her typing.

Autumn walked out of the office, but instead of taking a right to head towards the elevator, she turned left instead and walked to the stairs. She didn't care that they were so many floors up and her heels were not meant to take that kind of abuse. She just didn't want to risk running into Xander one more time today. She'd embarrassed herself enough for one week.

When she got home, she changed into a pair of soft, well-worn jeans, thick, fuzzy socks, poured herself a glass of wine and carried all of her work onto the back patio. Today was warm enough, but by the time night arrived, it would most likely be too cold to sit out here. So she took advantage of the sunshine while she could.

She curled up on her extra-large chair and pulled her laptop out. But that was as far as she made it in her quest to finish up the project she'd been working on earlier today. Instead of focusing on the report about employee productivity Ryker had asked for, she stared into space, not even remembering the wine she'd poured that was warming by her elbow.

"I thought you said you were working at home," a deep voice said from her doorway.

Autumn's head whipped around and her mouth fell open when she spotted Xander standing in her doorway. "What are you doing here?" she asked, standing up quickly but she forgot about all the papers that she'd spread out around her and the computer she'd had balanced on her knees. The papers slipped down from the cushions but she couldn't stop them since she was trying so hard not to let the expensive laptop hit the stone patio.

Before she knew what was happening, Xander was there on his knee as well, grabbing papers and computer. She looked up, right into his eyes and realized that he was closer than she'd thought.

There was a long, tense moment when her eyes went from his and then down to his mouth. And then she remembered what had happened earlier today when she'd done that and she took a deep breath and pulled back. "What are you doing here?" she asked again.

He smiled that charming grin that always made her stomach flutter. "I knew you'd need help catching all of these papers," he explained, "so I rushed over as quickly as I could." She used to love that smile, she thought. Initially, she'd thought he reserved that smile just for her. He'd tease her in the lobby or when they accidentally run into each other in the hallways. But then she'd seen him use it on one of the women that showed up in the office to collect him. And that smile, directed towards another woman, had shown her that he spread that smile around to everyone and anyone.

She stepped back and sat down on the chair again, wishing he would stop doing this to her. "And the real reason?" she snapped at him, stuffing her papers into her bag again. She wasn't getting any work done today, why even pretend?

"Because Mary said you went home early and I wanted to check on you, make sure you were okay."

"I'm fine," she said and lifted her glass of wine to take a sip. Unfortunately, the white wine had been sitting by her elbow so long that it had gotten warm. Her face squinched up with disgust and she almost spit the wine back in.

"Too warm?" he asked, laughing at her funny expression as he took a seat across from her.

"Yes. It's disgusting," she replied, chuckling a little herself at how she must have looked.

"I'll get you some more," he said and stood up himself. "No, don't stress," he teased again. "I'll find your kitchen in here somewhere."

She couldn't stop the laughter that escaped her this time because he was teasing her about how small her townhouse was. She didn't care though. It was the perfect size for her. The monthly payments allowed her to put more away towards investments than she spent each month so that was an extra bonus.

He came back with not one glass filled with chilled white wine, but two. And the dratted man sat right back down across from her. "So now you can explain to me why you left work so early when you've never left work early before." His eyes narrowed suddenly as if something occurred to him. "In fact, when was the last time you took a vacation?" he asked gently.

She smiled and shook her head. "That's not fair since you rarely take vacation either. You can't condemn me when you're doing the same violation."

"Touché!" he came right back at her. "So start explaining."

He leaned back in the comfortable chair and watched her. She didn't answer his question, but they did have a lively debate about another issue, one he couldn't even remember and which segued from one topic to another. He didn't care either. He simply enjoyed being here with her.

They used to talk like this, he remembered. Until that bastard had come to pick her up for a date. He'd been so furious after seeing her with another man, he'd gone straight to the gym that night and knocked out one of his sparring partners. He hadn't been allowed back into the gym for a week after that incident.

Now she was here, the afternoon sun fading into darkness and he watched the light play off of her beautiful features. He liked her like this, relaxed, in her own domain and feeling more confident. He'd had a hard time lately. His mind vacillated between memories of her being hit by the brute and then the way she'd looked as she'd climaxed in his arms. He hadn't been sleeping well either because every time he fell asleep, he'd feel her again, only to wake up and find that she wasn't there.

It had been tough when he'd only fantasized about her being in his bed. Now that he had the reality as a memory, it was ten times worse. He wanted her back, in his bed and in his arms. And he wanted to figure out how to keep this camaraderie going. He wasn't sure if he could have both, but he was determined to figure out how. Their kiss this afternoon proved that she wasn't as immune to him as she was trying to pretend.

Xander couldn't believe how comfortable her backyard was with the small lights intertwined into the tree branches that came on automatically as they talked about everything and anything. He loved watching the animation on her beautiful features and thought he could spend the rest of his life just sitting here in her backyard watching her and listening to her talk about all of her hopes and dreams, arguing with him about politics, or just telling him he needed to get a grip on whatever he was arguing about with her.

He liked that about her. People didn't normally argue with him. His clients came to him furious with their spouse and told him to make the marriage that they'd worked so hard for just disappear. He told them what to do, how to protect themselves from their spouse's lawyer and they did it. They followed his instructions to the letter, never even questioning his expertise.

Autumn would argue with him about the sky being blue simply because that was who she was. And it turned him on like nothing else could. As the night slowly descended and the twinkle lights showed off her laughing, brown eyes, he had to shift in his seat to adjust his hardening body as he watched her.

Why had she run away the last time they'd been together? What had he done wrong? His other lovers over the years had told him that he was a good lover, and he knew with absolute certainty that she had enjoyed their night together. But ever since that morning, she'd pulled back, put space between them. It was as if she were now embarrassed that she'd given in to the temptation. Which really rankled since he hadn't regretted a single moment. Except, perhaps, that it hadn't lasted longer. Fifty years longer, he thought with irritation.

She shook her head about some political viewpoint he'd just discussed and told him point blank that he was wrong. He laughed, but didn't contradict her claim, enjoying the confidence that was such a part of who she was. She hadn't spoken to him like this in…years! Ever since she'd been the receptionist, not knowing what she wanted to do with her life. She'd been so fresh and eager back then. Well, she still was, he thought as she laughed at his comment about the latest politics. But there was something different about her now. A hardness about her eyes and her mouth that had evolved over the years. And every once in a while, he saw something in her eyes, a hurt that made his stomach clench. When he saw that look, no matter what angry words she was spewing in his direction, all he wanted to do was pull her into his arms and make her tell him who or what had hurt her. He wanted to protect her, to make her life happy and erase all the anger and frustration, except when it was directed towards him!

He picked up the bottle of wine, intending to fill up her glass again. He'd only had half a glass, enjoying her laughter too much to muddy his focus by drinking wine. But when he realized that it was empty, he knew that it was time to leave.

Hell, he didn't want to leave. He wanted to lift her into his arms and make love to her right here on the soft grass of her back yard. And then he wanted to carry her into her house and make love to her on every horizontal surface he could find.

"I'd better head home," he said instead of pulling her out of her chair so she would land on his lap. When she looked down at her hands instead of at him, begging him with those warm, chocolate eyes, he got the message. "Get out of here," he read in her body language.

Damn! After that kiss in the conference room, he'd thought that perhaps she might be as interested in exploring this chemistry he knew they were both experiencing. For so long, he'd wanted her. Initially, she'd been too young. Fresh out of college, wonder in her eyes and excitement at all the world had to offer her. He'd stayed away. But she wasn't fresh out of college any longer. And the way she'd looked at him earlier today after their kiss, not to mention the way she'd responded to his touch… No, he chided himself. She hadn't been herself that day. He'd taken advantage of her after the fight. He knew perfectly well how the adrenaline rushed through one's system after a fight and he'd kissed her right after that. She'd been reacting to the fight, not to him.

But this afternoon…there hadn't been any fight. There hadn't been any adrenaline. Well, until he'd walked away from her. He'd wanted to fight someone, to punch them so hard he could actually do damage when he'd had to walk away from that conference room.

With a sigh and a groan of determination, he rose from the chair. "I'll leave you alone now. But thanks for the wine," he said. "And I enjoyed talking with you. It was just like old times."

He got out of there as quickly as he could, almost running from the house now. Because if he didn't get out now, he wasn't sure he'd have the strength to do it later. Not when she was looking so sweet and sexy sitting there in the big chair, her legs curled underneath her with those cute pink socks. She always looked so sophisticated at work with those killer heels and her skirts so tight that they left nothing to the imagination where her legs or bottom were concerned.

Actually, correct that! Her butt was even better when it was uncovered, he remembered. He hurried faster, almost diving into his car before he changed his mind. He could easily convince himself to turn around and drag her into his arms. He could get her wanting him again. He was sure of it, but would that be fair? She didn't want him normally, so pushing his attentions on her was inconsiderate.

His tires almost squealed as he pulled out of her parking lot and drove home. His hands gripped the steering wheel, white knuckling it all the way home until he reached his apartment complex. When he finally reached his own place, he went straight to his great room and... stopped in his tracks.

"What the hell are all of you guys doing here?" he demanded as he realized all three of his brothers were sitting in his apartment. And they were drinking his best scotch!

"We're celebrating!" Ash called out, standing up and handing him a glass.

Xander didn't hesitate. He took the glass and downed the amber liquid, then held it out for his brother to fill it up again. "Why was my place the designated celebration zone?" he asked, downing the next glass as well.

"Because it was closest," Ryker responded as if that were the most obvious answer, lifting his glass up for Ash to fill it as well.

Xander sat down in one of the deep chairs, his brothers draped over his sofa or the other chair. "And?" he prompted, needing more of an explanation. Although, it wasn't like his brothers to need much of an explanation to celebrate anything. There had been occasions when they'd all congregated simply to celebrate Tuesday or whatever day of the week it happened to be.

All four of his brothers looked like he felt and they were all slamming down the scotch at an alarming rate. No one explained why they were celebrating, but they joked and teased each other just like brothers were prone to do. It felt good, drinking like this after being in Autumn's company. He needed the release, the ability to just kick back. It was either get drunk with his brothers or head right back to Autumn's townhouse, picking her up into his arms and making love to her against the wall. He didn't think she would be very receptive to that option so he kicked his feet up onto his coffee table, forcing himself to stay put.

He laughed as the four of them got drunk, ribbing each other for the way they lived their lives or the lack of a lady love in their lives. When that subject came up, Xander was silent, staring at the liquid in his drink while he thought about the most frustrating woman on the planet. He had women throwing themselves at him at social events, showing up at the office constantly. Rarely could a business meeting be conducted at a restaurant now because women would stop by his table, dropping barely veiled hints that he should ask them out, or not even bothering to wait, but offering themselves up for one party or charity event or another. It was irritating, especially since Autumn was the only woman he wanted on his arm.

"Well, it isn't like the resident monk would know anything about that," Axel was saying.

Xander had no idea what they were talking about, but he looked up and all three of his brothers were looking directly at him. "What?" he asked.

The three of them rolled their eyes. All of them knew about his infatuation with their office manager although none would come out and say it for fear of Xander's anger at the sensitive subject. But they also knew that Xander had rejected women's advances ever since Autumn had walked into their office and started working for The Thorpe Group.

"When was the last time you got laid?" Ash asked.

He wasn't about to tell any of his brothers about his afternoon and evening with Autumn that had surpassed all of his fantasies. They might be close personally and definitely professionally, but his relationship with Autumn was private. "You're a crude ass, did you know that?" he said. Turning to Ryker, he brought up another subject, not bothering to wait for an answer from Ash, nor did he expect one.

"Hey, whatever happened with that altercation in the deli where Autumn was hurt?" Ryker asked. "I got the police report, but I think the police were still waiting for you and Autumn to go down and make a statement."

Xander had completely forgotten to take Autumn down to the station. "Did that jerk get released?" Xander asked furiously, sitting up straighter in his chair. "If he so much as comes near her…" he left the sentence hanging since all three of his brothers were quick to reassure him that the culprit that had started the fight had been sentenced to community service and anger management classes as well as two years' probation.

In Xander's mind, he didn't think that was strong enough of a punishment, but he couldn't really go to the judge and demand something worse. The jails and prisons were packed already with criminals; they wouldn't pay much attention to a guy who took a swing at a woman.

Maybe Xander could. He mentally made a note to have their lead investigator, Mark, look into the guy's background. Anyone who was willing to pick a fight in a public place in the middle of the afternoon had to have some skeletons in the closet. Perhaps it was time to become the fellow's worst nightmare. In Xander's experience, someone like that had a lot more issues that had been swept under the rug. It was time to bring them out, make the man accountable, he thought with relish.

"Any idea why Autumn didn't fight the new accounting software decision today?" Axel asked, shooting for what he thought might be a less explosive subject.

Ryker looked over at Xander who was staring down at his glass. Xander had no idea that his brothers were waiting for a response. He was too caught up in his plans to make the brutish man's life a living hell. So when he lifted his glass to drain the remaining scotch, he realized that all three of his brothers were staring at him oddly.

"What?" he asked, standing up and pouring himself another glass of scotch. He needed something to dull the memory of Autumn, both last Monday as well as this afternoon when she'd looked so soft and warm sitting in her tiny but cozy backyard.

Ash chuckled at his brother's irritated expression. "We were talking about the staff meeting earlier today," he said. "Obviously you're as much aware of our current conversation as she was this morning."

Since the four of them had killed the first bottle, Xander was grabbing another from the sideboard where he kept the liquor. But at the first mention of the staff meeting, he dropped the bottle of scotch. The very meeting after which he'd kissed Autumn for the first time since he'd made love to her.

He looked up at the others warily, trying to hide his reaction. "What about it?"

Ash, Axel and Ryker all looked at each other curiously, then back at Xander who was wiping up a puddle of thirty year old scotch before he got another bottle out from his stash. "What's going on?" Axel asked, voicing what was on everyone's mind.

"Nothing," he snapped back and slapped the next bottle of scotch down in the middle of the coffee table so no one had to exert any effort to get up to pour their next round. Himself included. "Why do you ask?" Had he revealed something? He didn't want to do anything to make Autumn feel uncomfortable. Their afternoon and evening together was their private secret. If anyone knew, she'd feel awful. She'd never said it in so many words, but he knew her well enough that it would be an issue in her mind.

Ryker raised an eyebrow. "You didn't think it was strange that the accounting software was approved?"

Xander shrugged and took another sip, not looking any of his brothers in the eye.

Ash tilted his head as he said, "The less expensive software? The one she didn't want us to get?"

Xander's hand froze in mid-air with that news. Had that really happened during the meeting? Damn! He'd really been out of it. He'd been watching Autumn during the meeting, noticing that she was unusually silent. Obviously, he hadn't been very attentive to the meeting agenda. "I think she had something else on her mind. We'll have to run it by her again next week."

Ash laughed and shook his head. "I can't imagine what she was thinking about," and looked over at his brother, trying to prompt him into a reaction. But after so many years of taking sides, Xander was silent. Another indication that something important was going on.

Ash glanced at his brothers, concern written on all of their faces as they surveyed Xander's silence.

Xander knew exactly where this was going. "Not going to talk about it. I have no idea what's on her mind," he said honestly. She might be thinking that their liaison together had been fantastic and she didn't want to ruin it by a second go, or she might have thought he was a complete ass. He had no clue. "So don't give me that look."

"Did you fight with her this week?"

Xander laughed. "Actually, this is the first week we haven't fought about anything." Which, in itself, was odd.

"Do you think she was more badly hurt in that fight than she's letting on?" Ash asked, concern obvious in his eyes.

Xander thought about that, remembering the way she'd moved while in his arms on Monday after the altercation. Yes, she'd been bruised. No, she wasn't more wounded than they all thought. He ruthlessly suppressed his body's reaction to those images and quickly shook his head. "She's not physically hurt. As for mentally?" He shrugged, honestly not sure what her mental state was at this moment. He couldn't even guess which, was part of the problem.

They moved away from personal issues after that. Apparently, all of the brothers were wary of discussing what was going on in their lives and they fell into their old habit of teasing each other over the cases they were handling.

By the time midnight rolled around, all of them were too drunk to head home so each of them found their respective bedrooms while Xander fell into his own bed. But even all the scotch he'd imbibed during the evening hadn't dulled his need for the one woman who constantly drove him crazy. Who had driven him insane with need for years.

Something was going to have to give, he thought. He wasn't sure how much longer he could be a gentleman about the woman. Perhaps he would start his own firm somewhere. Far away from Chicago so he wouldn't be tempted by her sexy figure in those killer heels every day of his life.

Hell, maybe he should just let her move her office to another floor! She'd tried to do that several times in the past but he'd simply vetoed her arrangement, configuring the office assignments so she was still on his floor. He smiled as he stared up at the ceiling of his darkened bedroom, thinking of the time when he'd arranged it so that her office was right next to his. He chuckled in the darkness. She'd only let that set up last for a few months before she finally created a reason to move her office back down the hallway from him.

Across the city, Autumn was laying in her own bed in the exact same position. She'd finished crying about the way Xander had almost run out of her townhouse earlier tonight. The final insult had been when his tires had squealed on his way out of her driveway.

The man had been desperate to get away from her! How pathetic was she that he needed to speed away like that?

She wiped her cheek angrily, irritated that she was still crying. No more, she told herself firmly. She was finished trying to figure this out. She had to figure out how to get Xander out of her heart. They'd had one fabulous, incredible and amazing night together. Even his kiss this afternoon had made her toes curl with desire. But enough was enough. She wanted kids and a husband while Xander had a daily, front row seat watching people tear each other apart.

At this point in his life, he probably didn't believe in marriage. And she didn't blame him. He'd seen the worst and had avoided the state for so long despite numerous women trying to get him to the altar. She had no chance to succeed where so many others had tried and failed.

Xander was probably right to avoid both commitment and matrimony.

That didn't help her heartache a whole lot though.

Sniffing into the darkness, she knew what she had to do. But even the thought of leaving The Thorpe Group made her whole body ache with sadness. She'd worked so hard to get things to their current state of efficiency. She didn't know if she had the energy to start over somewhere else.

But what was the alternative? She couldn't stay so that only left the option of leaving. It was better to just get out of the situation rather than die a slow death by watching him every day.

CHAPTER 6

Thursday night, Xander was working late in his office. He was tired, irritated by a lack of progress on certain cases, his brothers were looking at him strangely and he hadn't seen Autumn all day today. He realized at this moment how much just the sight of her helped him get through the day. When she passed by his office or he saw her in the kitchen or a conference room, it made him feel good. He might not be able to hold her in his arms, but her smile warmed his heart.

Xander tossed the paper to the side of his desk, rubbing his forehead wearily. He was irritated with a client he'd met with earlier in the day who was demanding everything from her husband. The husband had supported his client for the past twenty years, giving her just about anything she wanted. The woman had a huge house on Lake Shore Drive, spent her days shopping and eating in the best restaurants with her friends, throwing elaborate parties, not many of which were for her husband's business connections. Hell, she walked around with a five thousand dollar purse on her wrist and two thousand dollar shoes.

Her husband had cheated, which Xander didn't condone, but now the woman wanted everything in the settlement. But it wasn't in Xander's nature to be unfair. In this case, he suspected that the woman was either having an affair, or didn't even care that her husband had cheated on her. In his opinion, she was only using this as an excuse to divorce him and take him for everything.

He was leaning back in his chair, trying to figure out how to convince his client to leave her husband with at least one set of clothes and a few bucks in his bank account when he heard a noise. It was late enough that the office should be cleared out. There were always the superstar lawyers that were trying to impress by staying later than the boss, but this was going too far, he thought. Everyone needed balance in their lives and staying in the office working until ten o'clock at night was ridiculous.

Getting up, he followed the sounds, finally locating the late nighter in the copy room. And in this particular case, he didn't mind the person working late. Not one little bit.

Leaning against the metal door frame of the copy room, he watched with fascination as Autumn walked barefoot from the copier to the work counter, collating charts and graphs. He had no idea what case she was working on or what system she was going to try and convince the four of them to buy into next. All he cared about was watching her, fascinated by her cute toes that curled up against her calf as she tried to relax the muscles in her legs.

She was shorter than he'd thought. It shouldn't have been such a surprise, since she always wore three inch heels to give everyone a false sense of her actual height. But without heels, he suspected she wouldn't even come up to his shoulder.

She was singing something to herself and it occurred to him that he didn't even know what kind of music she preferred. It sounded a bit like a country song he'd heard recently, but he wouldn't bet on it. Autumn might know how to run an office like a well-oiled machine, but she couldn't carry a tune to save her soul.

"What are you doing here so late at night?" he asked and enjoyed her startled expression. He wished he was closer to her so he could have grabbed her to steady her. He'd use just about any excuse to touch her. Hell, he'd use almost any excuse just to see her. The woman had been avoiding him lately.

"What?" Autumn asked, her eyes searching frantically for someone else to magically appear behind him. Please don't let them be alone, she thought to herself.

He stepped into the room, watching her back up slightly as he approached. "I asked what you were doing here," he repeated. He glanced down at the graphs and smiled. "Are those the results from the survey?" he asked. She'd done an employee survey that he'd initially thought was ridiculous but as soon as she'd explained her reasoning, he'd agreed that it was an important project. That hadn't stopped him from arguing with her. He'd done so only so he could walk into her office and start the confrontation over again after the meetings.

Autumn squared her shoulders and tried to hide the results from Xander. "Yes, as a matter of fact, it is the results. I know you are opposed to silly things like employee morale and trying to ensure that good employees stay with the firm, but I know there are many things we can do to improve the way we do things here, to help people want to stay besides simply giving them more money."

Xander chuckled, loving the way she defended her ideas so passionately. "I agree with you," he said and moved even closer.

Autumn held her breath, leaning back against the work table and barely able to grasp the meaning of his words. "You do?" she asked, feeling like the air had been knocked out of her lungs.

"I do. And I'm very grateful to you for bringing the idea to us, as well as ensuring that the project was put out to all the employees in such a professional and thoughtful manner."

Autumn blinked, completely confused now. "I thought you didn't believe in wasting time and resources on employee morale surveys," she said softly.

"That was then," he lied. "This is now." And he moved closer. He watched her carefully, waiting for some sort of sign. He'd seen it that day in the conference room and he'd acted on it. He hadn't gotten any signals from her that afternoon in her backyard, but maybe he hadn't been paying attention well enough.

He was paying attention now!

When her mouth softened, he moved closer. When he saw her eyes drop to his mouth, he shifted so that his arms were braced behind her on the wall. He wasn't touching her in any way, but when her head tilted back, he couldn't resist leaning his head down and touching those soft, full lips. And when he felt her sweet breath on his mouth, he couldn't stop himself from deepening the kiss.

Autumn couldn't believe how badly she wanted Xander to kiss her. No matter how many times she told herself to avoid this man, when he came close to her, she couldn't banish this need. Damn him! Why wasn't he kissing her? What did a woman have to do to get him to kiss her?

Unable to stop the reckless need down deep inside of her, she lifted her hands, her palms flattening against his chest then sliding upwards. That seemed to be the only signal he needed because his arms wrapped around her, almost crushing her as he lifted her against his body.

"Damn you feel good," he said through gritted teeth as he lifted her up and slid her back onto the table behind her. "And you look adorable without your shoes on," he told her, his hands sliding down her hips, then back up and underneath her tight skirt, bringing the material higher.

"Xander, we can't…" she started to say, but then his hand touched the bare skin at the top of her thigh high stocking and she gasped, unable to speak. Her mouth dropped open, her eyes closed and her head rolled backwards while her hands balanced her weight behind her so she could lift her leg up higher, giving him better access.

"Tell me you want me," he commanded her, his fingers fluttering along her skin, his eyes fascinated by the expression of bliss on her face and his body was already hard and ready to plunge into her heat. He'd wanted her so badly ever since that one night. He'd pushed it out of his mind, thinking it had been a fluke. But then the kiss in the conference room…ah, he'd never forget her response.

Now she wasn't going to get out of it. He wouldn't allow her to deny what they felt for each other. Just the look on her face told him what he wanted to know, but he wanted her to tell him in words. He wanted to hear her say it.

"What do you want?" he coaxed, his fingers discovering the edge of her lace underwear. "Tell me," he commanded.

His other hand slowly worked the buttons on her silk blouse, leisurely revealing the nude colored lace holding her perfect breasts in place. Just for him, he thought. The peaks were already hard, already calling to him. He bent over her and kissed her neck, nibbling on her collar bone while his fingers down lower teased her hips and her breasts.

Autumn thought she might just go up in flames. With his lips and hands teasing her, she was so primed to climax she just…. "To the right," she whimpered.

His dratted hand moved to the left and she bit her lip as her hips shifted that way as well. Arching her back so that his fingers would claim more of her breast, she shook her head as the feelings drove her almost insane with need. "Please Xander!" she inhaled, her hips lifting, needing his fingers just slightly over to the right.

"Tell me you want me," he commanded again, nibbling on her earlobe.

"We can't," she sighed and shook her head back and forth.

"We can and we are. As soon as you say the words," he whispered in her ear.

In frustration, she grabbed his wrist, intending to move his hand where she so desperately needed it but he chuckled and pulled his hand away. Since he was much stronger than she was, there was nothing she could do. "I want you!" she gasped out, needing him so badly. "I need you inside me right now!" she finally said, her eyes open with anger, or passion, shining through her irises.

Xander swallowed hard, his body throbbing with need now. She was right where he wanted her and she'd actually said the words. And those words freed him, gave him all the permission he needed.

"Take off your underwear," he told her almost harshly. When she didn't move fast enough, he ripped them off for her. He opened several buttons on his shirt then took her hands and splayed her fingers over his chest. "Touch me," he told her while he grabbed something out of his back pocket and quickly adjusted his clothing.

With rough hands, he pushed her skirt up around her hips and her silk blouse down off of her shoulders. When that wasn't enough, he almost ripped her bra down so her breasts were freed to his hungry eyes. He bent her back over his arm, holding her in place so his mouth could devour her breasts. He wasn't gentle, his mouth covering her nipple and sucking hard, causing her to scream out and her hips to shift, needing his fingers back where they had been. Xander didn't disappoint. With one hand holding her in place for his mouth, his other hand moved lower, his fingers sliding into that heat that had been tempting him for the past several minutes.

"You're so wet for me," he growled. His fingers came out of her and he heard her whimper once again but her hips weren't still. They were seeking, her whole body arched in preparation for his invasion.

"Open your eyes, Autumn," he told her. When she wasn't fast enough, he yelled at her again. "Now!"

When she followed his command, he held her eyes while he pushed into her. Gently at first, but as she wiggled against him, adjusting her body to absorb his whole length, when he was fully embedded inside of her, he held her eyes while he pushed into her. He wasn't gentle now. He needed her too painfully and the way she was pressing against him was driving him more crazy.

He put her hands on his shoulders then dropped his hands down to her hips, holding her in place while he pounded himself into her, shifting to give her as much pleasure as possible and watching her eyes the whole time, just to make sure he wasn't hurting her.

"Now, Autumn," he coaxed, pressing himself tighter and he held on to that last, tiny thread of control so that she could experience every pulsating second of pleasure possible. He loved the way her body throbbed around her as her orgasm swamped over her, her eyes closed and her body arched, her legs gripping him hard and she cried out with her ecstasy. When he couldn't hold back any longer, his own climax washed over him and he thought he'd rather die than ever leave this moment with Autumn wrapped around him more tightly than he'd ever thought possible.

She had no concept of time or how long they'd been here. She felt like she was floating on a cloud of happiness. Autumn sighed cheerfully, her fingers drifting down over Xander's muscular shoulder to his chest...then lower. She laughed when he growled and grabbed her hand.

"You want another round?" he asked and bit her neck.

Autumn couldn't help the giggle that escaped her and she tried to move away, but since they were still intimately connected and he was much, much stronger than she was, he held her in place.

But then reality started to come back and her mind began to question why something was hard against her back. Looking around, she gasped as she noticed the copier and all the equipment around her.

"Oh no!" she groaned and started pushing against his broad, muscular shoulders, trying not to let her fingertips touch him. If that happened, she wasn't sure she would have the ability to resist the temptation to touch him further.

"What's wrong?" he asked, moving away slightly and helping her sit up.

"We had sex in the copy room!" she whispered frantically, trying to push her skirt down and button her blouse at the same time. She had absolutely no idea where her underwear was! How embarrassing.

Dressing would have been difficult to begin with but her bra was all out of place as well and that added a third layer of complexity.

Xander looked down at her as she tried to dress, adjusting his own clothing while he chuckled at her frantic movements. "Why are you whispering?" he teased, taking over the task of fixing her bra. But she only smacked his hands away when he started taking it off of her more than he was trying to put it back on.

"I'm whispering because I don't want anyone to hear us if they are still in the office! Do you know how horrible it would be if we were caught having sex in the copy room?" she hissed.

Xander's eyes widened with understanding at her reasoning. "Honey, if anyone were still here, they would have heard you a few minutes ago. You definitely weren't quiet then."

She blushed at the memory and glanced at him, surprised that he was already hard and ready for another go. "Please don't tell me that turns you on," she sighed as she finally got her clothes back in order. Or somewhat in order.

He laughed as he slid his tie off of his neck. She'd tossed it behind his shoulder during their lovemaking but he didn't think he needed it any longer. "Are you kidding me?" he asked, astonished that she would even question how turned on he was. It was pretty evident. "Nearly everything about you turns me on."

She was about to start picking up her reports, but her body froze with those words. "Everything?" she asked softly, staring up at him. Was he lying to her? Was this just another one of his lines that he told all the women? Xander was one of those charming men who knew all the right things to say to make a woman feel special and feminine. Had he learned that particular line worked exceptionally well? Because it was definitely making her body warm up, even if it was just a line.

Xander smiled softly and took her hands in his. She only resisted for a moment before she stood up and let him pull her into his arms. "I'll admit this resistance to seeing me, avoiding me in the hallways isn't very exciting. But when I do see you, and get a glimpse of your long, sexy legs in your ultra-sophisticated skirts and those heels – yes, that turns me on." He bent and nuzzled her neck and smiled to himself when her arms reached up to lay gently on his shoulders. "And when I think about what you wear underneath those silk shirts and stiff suits, I sometimes have to go back to my office and hide out until I can get my body back under control." He let his hands slide up her waist, cupping her perfect breasts in his hands, even enjoying the silk of her blouse when he knew that the silk of her skin was even softer.

"We can't do this," she sighed, leaning her head back and pressing her body against his, loving the differences in the way they were made.

"Yes we can," he countered and bit her earlobe.

She shivered, but still managed to shake her head. "No. It would be embarrassing."

He wasn't sure why it would be embarrassing, but he didn't want her to feel uncomfortable. "We're not going to ignore this anymore Autumn," he warned as he moved his hands down to her bottom, pressing her hips more closely to his own. "And I want to know why you walked away from me last week."

She took a deep, shuddering breath, trying to focus. "I need space if we're going to talk about this," she finally said, unable to think when he was holding her so tightly.

He grinned as he leaned down at nibbled on her lower lip. "Then maybe I won't stop touching you," he replied and kissed her, teasing her until she kissed him back. When he lifted his head, she was clinging to him, exactly how he liked her to be.

She laughed nervously, terrified of how easily he could make her want him. "I refuse to be the latest office bet," she said firmly as she pulled out of his arms.

He shifted so he could see her more clearly. "What are you talking about?" he asked, his hands still moving along her body.

Autumn sighed with irritation which was just a mask for how badly she wanted to slide right back into his arms. "Don't you ever go into the kitchen to get a cup of coffee?"

"Sure. What does that have to do with anything?"

She rolled her eyes. "The paper on the fridge?" she prompted then waited a moment for him to get it. But his eyes were still blank. "It's the office betting pool for your current lady love," she finished.

His hands stilled. "What do you mean?"

She pulled out of his arms and moved to the opposite side of the copy room. "The entire office bets on how long your current lover will last. When a new woman shows up, a new pool starts. Hence the new dates, the initials by each of those dates...." She prompted, hoping he would get the picture.

He thought about those for a moment, then shook his head. "You're kidding, right?"

She shook her head, trying to hide the pain she felt every time a new paper went up onto that fridge. "Not at all. When the dates are all filled up, the paper is taken down and someone is assigned control of the money. It's currently five dollars a date," she explained.

Xander threw back his head and laughed, completely amused by the idea of his entire staff betting on how long a woman would stay in his life. Especially since there hadn't really been any woman in his life for so long.

Autumn took that time to gather up her materials, irritated and indignant that he would be amused by someone betting on his personal life. Not a good idea when he was asking to make her the next woman in his personal life. That was SO not going to happen.

Xander knew that his laughter was creating more problems, but he couldn't stop. It was so hilarious that his staff was betting, winning and losing money, on something that wasn't actually happening! Almost from the moment Autumn came to work from The Thorpe Group, the women in his life had been temporary only because he wouldn't, couldn't, give them what they wanted, a real relationship. The ladies became frustrated with how little he would communicate with them, how he barely even kissed them goodnight. Some of them even asked if he was gay because he was so disinterested when they tried to tempt him.

He'd tried often enough, desperate to get Autumn out of his mind. But none of them could compare to her innocent beauty or the energy and passion she put into everything she did. He loved watching her work, getting involved in whatever might not be working perfectly and making it better. She was like the efficiency energy bunny. He'd been entranced from the moment she'd walked in and sat her adorable butt down in the receptionist chair and he'd become more enraptured by her ever since.

But he could see how she might not want to become the latest office gossip. And he would probably need to ease her into the relationship he wanted from her. And then another thought occurred to him. "Are you seeing someone now?" he demanded, furious at the very idea of another man touching her.

She quickly shook her head, which relaxed his muscles again. "Good." He moved closer to her. "So if you don't want the rest of the staff to know that we're seeing each other," and he put a hand over her mouth when she immediately opened hers to argue with him, "And we will be seeing each other," he told her firmly. She stiffened for a moment and he watched her eyes. There was resistance for a long moment, then it seemed like she was accepting his statement so he released her mouth. "How about if we keep the office gossips from knowing about our relationship?" That would give her an easy out if she discovered that she didn't really like him as a man. Okay, so she liked him as a man if her reaction a few minutes ago was any indication, but she might not like him as a person and keeping it quiet would help her if she wanted out. But it would at least give him some time to be with her, to hold her in his arms and enjoy her company. He'd have to figure out how to not pressure her though. That didn't mean he wouldn't do everything in his power to convince her.

"What do you propose?" she asked, thinking she was a fool to even consider a relationship, secret or otherwise, with Xander Thorpe. He was a ladies man, through and through. He was jaded about relationships. He rarely spent any time with a woman before moving on to the next one that caught his eye because, in his mind, relationships didn't last. But maybe she could just take what he gave and tuck those memories into her mind for the future.

He grinned at her response. "We won't let anyone in the office know that we're together. We'll meet at your place or mine and get to know each other."

She wasn't sure she liked the idea. Well, she definitely loved the idea of being with Xander even if it was only temporarily. But the secret thing might be difficult to maintain. "And in public? Or at the office?"

"We can be cordial to each other, right?" he teased.

She bit her lower lip, trying to decide how big of a fool she was going to be when she agreed. Everything in her told her to reject the offer. It was insanity and she couldn't believe it when she said, "Okay."

She was rewarded by his grin which sent shivers throughout her whole body, filling her with decadent anticipation.

"So it's already Thursday," he said, moving closer one more time. "Are you going to come home with me tonight?"

She tried to take a deep breath, but his hands moved to cup her breasts again and it turned into more of a gasp. "It's late," she finally got out although it was hard.

"And?" he asked as if that weren't a good enough excuse.

Autumn knew what he wanted to hear, but she couldn't be that brazen. She wanted to tell him to take her home to his house or hers and start all over on what they'd just done, but this time in private. And slower. More thoroughly.

But she wasn't that confident around him.

He realized where her mind was going and finished his thought for her. "And you should come home with me so we can finish what we started again."

She shook her head and pushed against his shoulders. "If I go home with you, we won't get any sleep." Her nudge wasn't very convincing since she didn't want to sleep alone tonight. Good grief, she didn't even want to sleep!

He laughed, his hands moving higher on her waist. "I don't see a downside to that."

She thought frantically, trying to figure out what was good and bad about the whole situation. She knew this wasn't going to work, but her body wanted him so badly. "You have Ms. Goswin coming in at eight o'clock tomorrow morning."

He groaned at the reminder and his hands stilled although she felt his fingers clench on her hips. "That woman!" he snapped.

Autumn couldn't help but laugh. She'd never seen him express any kind of irritation with any of his clients. They all seemed to love him and he loved them. Some of them were repeat clients, which was truly crazy, but others considered

Xander a personal friend after their divorce was finalized. Autumn didn't want to know which of those offers he accepted.

"I thought you and Ms. Goswin were friends."

He quickly shook his head. "Can't stand her," he explained. "She's not a very nice person," he said in a low, irritated voice.

This was a new side to the man and she had to admit that she was amazed.

He looked around, still wanting to figure out how to get her back to his place and into his bed. "How about if I help you clean all this up and then I can take you home?"

She automatically bent to pick up the reports that had fallen to the floor during their bout of passion, trying to hide her blush at the mess that was all over the floor now. "I have my car here," she said as she grabbed all of the papers on her side of the copy room work table while he pulled together the ones on his side.

"It's late and you shouldn't be driving home at this time of the night alone."

She laughed and shook her head. "That's a crazy excuse and you know it."

He laughed as well and they both stood up with all of the gathered papers. "Yes, but it will get me closer to your bed, which is where I want to be."

"It will also leave my car here."

"I don't mind driving you into the office tomorrow morning."

"But everyone will see my car here. And some might see us driving in together. My name would be at the top of the kitchen pool paper by nine o'clock tomorrow morning."

He sighed, realizing what she was saying. "Okay, good point. So follow me home. That way, you'll still have your own car."

Again, she shook her head. "I'm going home alone tonight, Xander." She was proud of herself for being so firm about this.

"Then leave work early tomorrow and come with me. I'll show you my lake house and we can spend the whole weekend together."

Her eyes widened. "You have a lake house?" she asked, interested despite herself.

He shrugged slightly. "Only my brothers know about it," he said. "It isn't big, but it suits my needs."

She smiled, intrigued by yet another side of him. "And what needs are those?" she asked, more than a little curious.

"Privacy."

Her eyes widened. "I thought you were more of an extrovert."

"Normally, I like being around people, but every once in a while, I need the silence of nature." He looked at her cautiously. "I'm not kidding. It's pretty small and rustic."

She loved the idea but didn't want to appear too enthusiastic for fear of putting him off. She had to play it cool, she thought. "What time would you like to leave?" she asked.

He grinned right back at her. "Can you get out of here after lunch? It takes about two hours to reach the house so that will give us plenty of time to get out of here and head to the lake so it won't feel like the weekend is already gone."

She nodded her head, smiling shyly now that she knew his secret. "So that's where you go when you leave here early on Fridays," she said with a grin. "I can be ready tomorrow. And yes, I can get everything cleared off of my desk by lunch time."

"Great," he said. "I'll walk you to your car," he told her as he took her hand and led her back to her office where they both dumped all of the reports.

She grabbed her purse and her coat, leaving the rest of her work on her desk. There was no way she'd get anything else done tonight. She needed a shower and a bed. Preferably his, but she had to be firm about this and sleep in her own bed tonight. Tomorrow, there would be plenty of time to be in his arms.

CHAPTER 7

Autumn nervously packed her bag, not exactly sure what to include but she stuffed a couple pairs of jeans in, a bathing suit, some shorts and a sweater along with both long sleeve and short sleeve shirts. She included makeup, but only because she knew she wouldn't be ready to face Xander without any makeup yet. She might need, oh…maybe ten years, before she would have the courage to face the man with a fresh face. He was too suave and sophisticated and she couldn't imagine sitting across the table from him without looking her best.

She threw her bag into her trunk, then bit her lip as her mind worked through the details. She couldn't leave her car at the office because then everyone would know that she'd left with someone else. But she didn't want to waste time coming all the way back to her place. She lived about thirty minutes away, in the opposite direction from his place. Maybe he wouldn't mind if she left her car in the parking lot of his building, which was only about five minutes from their office.

With that settled in her mind, she dumped her bag in the trunk and slammed it shut.

All morning, she scrambled to get her desk cleared off. Every time she received a new e-mail, she jumped on top of the issue, eager to get it taken care of so no one would be upset by her leaving early. When her phone rang right before lunch, she jumped and glared at it, initially thinking it was another task to get cleared up. But then she saw Xander's extension, she smiled with relief and answered the phone.

"Are you still able to get out of here in say…an hour?" he asked.

"I'll be ready," she replied, feeling silly for the huge grin, grateful he couldn't see her.

"Good. I'll meet you in the lobby."

He was about to hang up when she stopped him. "Wait!"

"What's wrong?"

"Can I drive to your place and park at your apartment instead?"

There was a long pause and then he sighed. "Sure. That will work as well."

Autumn ended the call and turned back to her computer. There were three more messages that had come in just during that short conversation. She quickly opened all three and read through them, then quickly cleared up the issues that needed to be resolved.

Forty-five minutes later, she looked around. Her reports were collated and ready to be distributed, her e-mail was…well, not empty but all the major issues were cleared up, her desk was also clean of any major issues….

Was she really ready to go?

Her stomach flip flopped at the idea of a long weekend with Xander. There wouldn't be anyone around, just the two of them. Was she really going to do this? How stupid was it?

She should cancel, she thought. It was ridiculous to think that she would be any different from all the other women in his life. She would last just as long as they did and then she'd have to watch him with his next woman.

Could she handle that? Did she have the strength to endure him with another woman, knowing how she felt about the man?

Did she have a choice?

Not really.

Before she could come up with a reason not to, she grabbed her purse and headed out of her office.

"I'm leaving early today," she said to Mary, not seeing the surprise in her assistant's eyes as she swung her purse over her shoulder and headed out for the weekend. She was so embarrassed and nervous about what she was doing, afraid her guilt would be written all over her face, that she couldn't look anyone in the eye.

She told the receptionist that she was leaving as well and to talk to Mary if there were any problems, since the receptionist also worked for her as well. When Xander walked out just as she was reaching for the door handle, she cringed when he told the receptionist that he too was leaving early for the weekend.

They stood awkwardly in the hallway waiting for the elevator to arrive, not saying a word to each other. When the doors opened, Autumn stepped in and moved to the opposite side of the cab while Xander politely stepped back from the front to allow another woman to be in front of him.

Once outside the building, she walked to her car, got in and drove away without once looking in his direction. She noticed him pull out of the parking garage right behind her but she didn't even hesitate, too afraid someone from the office might be walking to lunch at one of the many restaurants along this street during their own lunch hour.

She pulled into the entrance of his building and, somehow, the gate for his building's parking garage quickly opened. She supposed he had some sort of electronic opener on his car but she was too nervous about what they were about to do to wonder about it too thoroughly.

She heard her phone ring and answered it from her steering wheel.

"Park in number three," Xander told her. She did so and he moved into space number one.

She was just gathering her purse when her car door opened up and Xander's strong, powerful hands were reaching in, lifting her up and into his arms. "That was ridiculous," he said a moment before he covered her mouth in a kiss that had her knees shaking so badly she couldn't even stand any longer.

When he lifted his head, their breathing was rough and rapid and she didn't want him to move away. In fact, if they weren't in a parking garage, she might be begging him to keep on going. She'd had trouble sleeping last night after his teasing touches and now that desire was right back, just as intense. Possibly more so because she knew what was going to happen.

"Get in my car," he ordered her with a heated look that told her he was just as on fire for her.

"Shouldn't I change clothes?" she asked, smiling. Or at least trying to smile. She wasn't sure she actually made it.

"If you even start to change clothes, I'll have them all off of you and we'll never get to my lake house. And I really want you where no one will be able to find either of us until Sunday night."

She could agree with that. So she pushed away from her car, her legs still pretty shaky, and slipped into his luxurious, black Jaguar sedan. The sleek lines of the exterior were mirrored on the inside and she loved the way the seat hugged her body, keeping her in place.

A moment later, Xander was right next to her and he was pulling out of the space.

"My clothes!" she gasped, forgetting that she needed her bag from her trunk.

"No need," he teased. But then relented when he saw her worried expression. "I got them out already. Your bag is in my trunk so there's no slowing down." He actually stopped at that point and looked at her in the dim light of the parking garage. "Are you sure about this, Autumn?" he asked gently, his hand touching her cheek, smoothing down to her jawline. "I don't want to pressure you into anything you don't want to do."

She almost laughed at that but he was being too sincere. "I guarantee that there isn't anywhere I'd rather be right now," she assured him.

Those beautiful, indigo blue eyes smiled right back at her and he drove quickly out of the garage. In only moments, they were speeding down the highway out of the city. They talked about everything and anything that occurred to them and Autumn couldn't believe how nice it was to have that camaraderie back that they'd had when she'd first started working at The Thorpe Group as a receptionist. He could make her laugh about the silliest things and yet, they argued about everything as well. The arguments this time were good natured, not nearly as heated as they had been before that afternoon in his penthouse. And she discovered things about him that she never would have believed.

The biggest surprise of all was two hours later when they pulled into a wooded, gravel driveway. This lake house wasn't anything like what she was expecting. While his penthouse in the city was gorgeous with all the latest gadgets and designer decorated, his lake house was the complete opposite. The house wasn't enormous and elegant. It was a small cabin, just like he'd told her. And it really was just a cabin. There were rough logs and stones and the edifice stood almost right on the water. The lake wasn't very deep right here, but it expanded out and looked cool and amazing farther to the right. There were pine trees behind the house and a perfect porch with two deep chairs that looked out onto the lake.

She didn't realize it, but Xander was standing behind her while she took it all in. When she just stood there, looking and not saying a word, he couldn't take the suspense any longer. "What do you think?" he asked.

Autumn didn't even turn her head. "It's perfect," she whispered, not wanting to raise her voice for fear that it might break the solemnness of the atmosphere. "How did you get such a perfect spot?" she asked.

He moved closer to her, wrapping his arms around her waist. "I bought up several lots up and down the lake from this point."

She rolled her eyes, shaking her head at how wealthy he was. "Only you," she laughed.

He squeezed her slightly then kissed her neck before releasing her. "Come see the inside."

She followed behind him, feeling warm and protected with his large hand holding hers. It felt like their first, real date, but that didn't make any sense after they'd known each other for so many years. Well, and the fact that they'd made love…um…had sex…so many times.

He led her down a dirt pathway towards the small cabin. There was a double door and a large window looking out onto the lake, but inside, there was only a rustic kitchen powered by solar panels on the roof. Nothing was turned on so Xander had to power up the fridge and small stove so it would at least be ready to use. There was a sitting area filled with deep, rough wood chairs surrounding the large, stone fireplace but not much else other than fishing and snow equipment against the wall. Other than that, there was only one bedroom with more rough wood as the bed and piles of blankets as well as one dresser and a closet in the corner.

"There's only one bedroom," she said as she backed up.

Xander looked down at her, his eyes confused. "Isn't that the whole point?" he asked, matching her step for step.

"Where am I going to sleep?" she asked.

Xander froze, his eyes trying to figure out if he'd completely misunderstood what was going to happen this weekend. Then he saw the teasing glint in her eyes and he growled. "You're not!" he told her in a deep, husky voice, ignoring her squeal as he bent low and tossed her over his shoulder.

Autumn was laughing so hard she could barely breathe but then she found herself on her back, staring up at the man and all her laughter died out while that delirious lust surfaced once more. The time for talking was gone. There was no teasing, no laughing. The only sound either of them made was gasping pleasure as clothes were pulled off and scattered, skin revealed and his hard body finding her softer one.

CHAPTER 8

The weekend was filled with laughter and exploration. Xander showed her all of his favorite places on the lake including a water fall, a secluded field that was filled with sunshine and hiking along the trails and into the forests. Since the water was still warm from the summer heat, he convinced her get into the water with him, but she refused to do it without her bathing suit. By the time they were back up on the front porch of his cabin, she was naked and desperate for him to take her, unconcerned about anyone seeing them because he'd gotten her to the point where she didn't care any longer.

When they weren't exploring the trails and lake, they were exploring each other. She'd never even known that men like Xander existed. He loved cooking and they competed with each other to make better pancakes, each making their own batch then sharing with each other. For dinner, he grilled the chicken and she made a potato casserole and salad. He opened a bottle of wine and they sat in front of the fire, eating, talking and sharing until she couldn't take his distance any longer and she crawled up onto his lap and made love to him the way she'd been thinking of doing ever since she'd seen the fireplace.

They talked and laughed, cooked and made love while intermittently exploring the outside world as well. By Sunday night, she didn't want to be without him, feeling addicted to his large body being so close to hers.

When they were back in the city late Sunday night, he tried to convince her to come up to his place and spend the night with him, but she remained firm in her desire to go home. She didn't have clothes to wear to work the following day and she didn't want to be late, which she would be if she spent the night in his arms and had to rush home the next morning to change.

"I'll make sure you're on time," he coaxed, nibbling on her ear until she was shivering again.

"You'll just keep me awake all night again and I'll be a walking zombie tomorrow, and I'll definitely be late because you might wake me up, but…" she didn't finish her sentence, blushing at the way he'd woken her up the previous two mornings.

He laughed and slipped his fingers underneath her flannel shirt. "You know I'm very good at waking you up," he told her, his sexy voice close to her ear.

"You're incorrigible," she said and sighed as she forced herself to slip out of his arms. She drove home that night but she tossed and turned, not able to fall asleep without Xander's arms around her and his body warming her own.

The following morning, she was late for work because she'd forgotten to put her alarm on and slept through when she would normally have gotten up.

She finally sat down at her desk only fifteen minutes late. When her phone rang at her elbow, she almost didn't answer it, knowing that it would be Xander. In the end, she was too desperate to hear his voice so she lifted the receiver, smiling when she heard his gloating voice.

"I told you to spend the night with me," he said softly and with that deep, sexy voice that she was becoming addicted to so quickly.

"How did you know I got into work late?" she asked, glancing to the open door of her office to make sure no one was coming in or might hear her.

"Are you kidding me?" he laughed. "I've been watching to see those long, sexy legs for the past few hours. I got in about six o'clock this morning."

"You did not!" she laughed, not believing him for a moment.

"It's true. I finally gave up on sleeping because you weren't there with me. By five this morning, I gave up and just came into the office."

She bit her lip since she'd had the same problem. "I…" she sighed, wishing she could be as open with him.

"I know, love. You had trouble sleeping too. But I'll fix that tonight," he said. "Have a good day today." And with that, he hung up, leaving Autumn shivering and smiling like an idiot.

Thankfully, the day flew by and Autumn was frantically trying to clear up the last few issues so she could head home. She wanted to get dinner started so she could surprise him tonight. She stopped and looked around, frozen with the realization that she was just assuming he would be coming to her house tonight.

Her cell phone buzzed and she glanced down, reading the text message. "Leave now!" was all it said.

She laughed out loud as she read it, but she also shut down her computer and grabbed her purse. She was just about to leave her office when she got a mischievous idea in her head. Instead of heading towards the lobby which would take her to the bank of elevators, she turned instead and headed towards the stairs. Xander would probably be heading towards the elevators now as well. He was probably anticipating catching her on the ride down to the parking garage.

She smiled as she waved goodnight to Mary and then disappeared into the stairwell. She slipped off her heels and sped down the stairs, hurrying as fast as her feet could take her. She knew she wasn't going to beat the elevator, but she wanted to beat Xander if at all possible. She had a plan in her mind. She wasn't sure she was brave enough to follow through though.

She was out of breath when she reached the bottom and sprinted to her car. Pulling out of the parking spot, she thought she saw Xander in a group of other people exiting the elevator, but she wasn't positive. She drove through traffic which, thankfully, was lighter at this hour. When she arrived home, she rushed up the stairs, pulled her hair up on top of her head and jumped into the shower. After taking a quick shower, she stood in front of her dresser with her underwear drawer open, now indecisive. If she were calculating things correctly, she didn't have much time left so she grabbed a black, lace bra and matching underwear, pulling them on quickly. She applied a bit more makeup, a pair of black heels (the pair that he'd bought her earlier that week), and stood in front of her mirror, surveying her appearance.

She was pacing back and forth in her room, her hands twisting together nervously. When the doorbell rang, she froze in place, staring at herself in the mirror one more time. Her heart was beating so hard, she could almost feel it in her pulse. But no matter how hard she tried, she simply couldn't answer the door in her black, lace underwear and heels.

When the doorbell rang a second time, she grabbed her robe and pulled it on, tying it tightly at the waist. "You couldn't have gotten a sexy, satin robe!" she admonished herself as she went down the wooden stairs to answer the door. "No, you have to get the frilly, flannel robe that makes you look like a creepy old maid with a hundred cats!"

She opened the door to find Xander on her doorstep. He looked angry and confused, and even surprised to see her.

"Are you okay?" he asked, still standing outside. His hands were on his hips and his broad shoulders looked tense.

Autumn's hands moved to cover herself. She might be wearing a robe, but she knew what she'd intended to be wearing and she suddenly felt vulnerable. He looked like he was now regretting his suggestion that they have an affair. Where was the voracious lover of the weekend? Had he had enough of her? Already? That was so unfair. Other women at least got several weeks with him. But he looked like he was trying to tell her he wanted out after only one weekend.

"I'm fine," she said, her hand gripping the belt of her robe. "Did you want to come in?"

He hesitated for a long moment before he said, "Do you want me to come in?"

Autumn thought she might just burst into tears. In fact, she felt the traitorous tears start to form in her eyes and she blinked rapidly to try and stop them.

Xander saw the look and the wetness in her eyes and he felt horrible. "Autumn," he groaned as he stepped inside her townhouse, his hands coming up to pull her against his chest. "I'm sorry, honey. I don't want to pressure you into something you don't want."

"What?" she gasped, pulling back so she could look up at him. "Something I don't want?" she repeated. "You looked like you were changing your mind."

He looked down at her, his hand moving from her back to cup her face, his thumb rubbing gently against her chin. "I didn't see you leave. I thought maybe you'd stayed at the office to try and avoid me. Then, when you opened the door, you looked irritated, almost angry to see me."

Autumn breathed in a shaky breath, letting her forehead fall onto his broad chest and almost laughed.

Xander didn't understand what was going through her head, but he was tired of trying to guess. "Autumn, if you don't want this, if you aren't feeling anything for me anymore, just say the word and I'll back off."

She laughed softly, but it came out sounding more like a hiccup because she was fighting both the release of her despair and the overwhelming joy that he still wanted her. "I still want you," she said against his shirt. She pulled back but still couldn't look up at him. "Very much so in fact," she whispered.

"Why did you look so sad when you opened the door then?"

One side of her mouth pulled away in an odd sort of grimace. "Because I was mad at myself."

He shook his head, still not understanding. "What's the issue?"

She sighed and stepped back, pulling at the tie to her robe. She couldn't look at Xander, fearful of the amusement she would see in his eyes. "You have women throwing themselves at you all the time. This is a bit harder for me," she finally said. When the tie was open, she held the edges closed with her hands.

"Autumn, I don't think you understand about those other wo…."

He was going to explain about the women in his life, but she slipped the robe off of her shoulders, letting it slither down her body to pool at her feet. Xander was speechless as he took in her slender body with only the black lace covering the important parts.

He didn't say a word. He stared. Hard. Autumn stood there, her nervousness increasing with his silence. Autumn couldn't take it any longer. She had to know what he thought. If he was laughing at her, she'd just shrug off his amusement and pretend to laugh with him.

Slowly, with absolute determination, she lifted her eyes to his.

She didn't see any amusement there. Only heat – and intensity – as he continued to look at her.

He cleared his throat slightly. "You rushed home to change."

"Yes," she whispered.

"You didn't rush back here to avoid me again."

Autumn was so surprised that he would think along those lines that she moved closer to him, relieved when his arms automatically wrapped around her body.

"You're beautiful, Autumn," he groaned a moment before his mouth covered hers in a kiss that demanded complete submission. She was more than willing to give it to him, thrilled that he still wanted her.

When he lifted her into his arms and carried her up the stairs, she wrapped her arms around his neck and laid her head on his strong shoulder, her body throbbing and excited in anticipation of his touch. And she wasn't disappointed. Xander was merciless, kissing every part of her body, teasing her and making her scream out with the need to find fulfillment. When he finally entered her, she sighed with happiness…until he started moving inside of her. Her fingers held on tightly, never wanting this moment to end. When it finally did end, she wasn't sad at all. Just thrilled that he was still here, in her arms. She snuggled close, smiling in the dim light filtering in through the hallway.

"I liked your surprise," he said as he wrapped his arms around her, pulling her back against his chest.

She laughed. "Maybe I'll get confident enough to actually open the door that way in a few years."

He chuckled as well. "I'll look forward to that evolution."

She thought it was sweet that he was even thinking he might still want her in a few years. And it warmed her heart whenever she thought back to the expression in his eyes when she'd dropped the robe. It gave her a bit more confidence sexually to know that he liked her figure that much.

"I'm hungry," she said several minutes later.

He lifted her hair off of her shoulder and nuzzled her neck. "I can oblige."

She laughed and shook her head. "For food," she clarified. She sat up in the bed and looked around, wondering where her robe was.

"It's downstairs on the hallway floor," he told her, reading her mind and then laughing when she bit her lip in consternation. "You're going to have to go down there naked to get it."

She looked at him over her shoulder, eyebrows raised as she accepted his challenge. She slid out of bed and Xander pushed up on his arms to watch, smiling slightly.

She sat on the edge of her bed, debating how she could do this. "It doesn't help if you're staring at me," she admonished him.

"What's the point of walking around your house naked if you don't let me watch?" he asked, pushing a pillow behind his head.

She couldn't figure out how to do it and looked at the floor, wishing she had a throw blanket on her bed she could wrap around herself. And then she smiled triumphantly when she spotted his white shirt on the floor.

"Oh, no you don't," he growled, realizing too late what she had planned. But he was too relaxed and that gave her the head start she needed. She whipped the shirt up off the floor and got her arms into the sleeves before he could stop her. The next thing she knew, she was running down the stair, laughing so hard she almost slipped on her robe when he chased after her, grabbing her by the waist and tossing her over his shoulder. She yelped when he smacked her bottom and trotted right back up the stairs.

"You cheated," he told her and tossed her into the middle of the bed. "For that, you're going to have to pay the price."

"What's the cost?" she gasped through her delighted laughter. But she didn't have long to wait. He kissed her, his body making her crazy.

Several hours later, she laughed as she pushed his hands away. "You can't touch me again until I get some food," she told him firmly. She stood up and grabbed her robe from the floor where she'd dropped it earlier, slipping her hands into the sleeves and tightening the belt around her waist. When she turned around, he was pulling on his jeans, buttoning the fly but he hadn't put on a shirt yet. Even after hours of being in his arms and finding fulfillment over and over again, the man could still stun her with the beauty of his muscular shoulders, chest and stomach. He was cut like a Greek statue and she considered telling him to get right back into bed.

Then her stomach growled and she knew she should focus on getting some food inside of her before anything else. "Right," she said out loud and padded barefoot out of her bedroom.

Xander watched her move, walking behind her so he could enjoy her from the back. "What are you making me for dinner?" he asked as they descended the stairs to the kitchen.

She snorted. "How about a peanut butter and jelly sandwich?" she suggested and opened the fridge.

He was looking in the pantry. "How about pasta?" he suggested and grabbed the jar of sauce and dried pasta. "You get the water boiling, I'll do the rest."

Her eyebrows went up with that. "I'll make the garlic toast," she offered and went into her freezer for the last half of the crusty bread she'd bought a while ago but hadn't used. There was a bit of cheese, fresh garlic and plenty of butter in the freezer which she kept on hand for when the mood struck to bake something yummy and decadent.

"You're on," he told her and reached around her to grab the vegetables that were in her fridge. "Stand back, woman," he said and started opening cabinets in search of the items he would need to make pasta.

For the next hour, they laughed and nibbled on vegetables while they cooked their dinner together. After they'd filled their stomachs with rich, cheese laden pasta, Xander pulled her back into his arms and made love to her once more before they fell asleep in each other's arms.

That started the pattern for the next several days. After work, they would meet at either his place or hers, they would cook, eat and laugh, enjoy each other's company and relax until he took her into his arms and made her so crazy with his touch and his kisses that she was begging him to take her. She had no idea if this kind of passion for another person was normal, but she suspected it wasn't. She'd heard others talk about sex with their spouses in the kitchen and what she was experiencing with Xander didn't have any resemblance to what others discussed. It was like apples and asparagus.

She was walking into the office, feeling happier than she ever had. Until she came face to face with her reality. "He said he had to work last night," a woman draped in a black dress was saying to Diane.

Autumn was about to walk by when something inside her told her to stop and linger for a moment.

"I don't know if he was working late last night, ma'am. But he hasn't come in yet today. Would you like to leave a message?" Diane asked in her kindest voice, which told Autumn that the black clad woman had already been her for a while and was making a stink about something.

"Can I help you?" Autumn asked, stepping forward to help Diane out of the situation.

The woman turned around, swinging her silky black hair in an arc to face the new voice. The woman looked Autumn up and down, dismissing her as unimportant. "I'm looking for Xander Thorpe," the woman explained. "I'm Marcy Duprey."

Autumn waited, expecting the woman to continue. When she finished with just her name, as if that were supposed to mean something, Autumn plastered her 'office manager' smile onto her face. "Do you have an appointment with Mr. Thorpe?" Autumn asked, her stomach starting to twist into knots. She knew exactly where this was going. Had known it would happen but wished it had taken more time.

"I don't need an appointment," the woman stated, preening slightly with a superior expression on her beautiful features. "And I'm just here to hear from him if the rumors are true."

Autumn swallowed, painfully aware that this woman might not be exaggerating. She'd left Xander's house only an hour ago but already she felt cold and rejected. "Mr. Thorpe isn't in the office at the moment. If you'd like to sit down and wait, I can bring you a cup of coffee. Or I can make an appointment for later in the day?" she offered, trying to sound normal and professional, but she suspected she was coming across as brittle and vulnerable, which is how she felt.

The woman waved the option away. "No need. I just need a moment of his time."

"Then you're going to wait?" Autumn asked.

Marcy laughed. "Goodness no. I've been waiting enough for that man. I'm not waiting any more. Besides, if what I read was true, then he has a lot to explain!" She slung her hair over her shoulder and walked out. With one hand on the door, she turned back. "Tell him to call me the moment he gets in," she ordered as if Autumn and Diane were her underlings, here to follow her commands.

Diane blew out her breath and slumped into the back of her chair. "That woman did not look happy."

Autumn knew the feeling. She'd been on top of the world only five minutes ago. The presence of that horrible woman had ruined that wonderful feeling she'd left the house with earlier.

Walking into her office, she had to control the urge to slam the door. She walked carefully and precisely to her desk and dove into the work. She pushed herself harder than ever that day, needing to push the image of that woman out of her mind.

"Did you hear?" Diane stepped into her office, excitement obvious in her eyes.

"Hear what?" Autumn asked, pulling the report off of the printer, her eyes scanning the details to ensure their accuracy.

"Mia Paulson is free! The police were even here to re-arrest her on embezzlement charges but some woman with Ryker recognized the alleged victim."

"You're kidding!" Autumn demanded, standing up and moving out of her office. "Where is she?"

"Down in Ash's office," Diane called back to her.

Autumn didn't wait any longer, running down the stairs to Ash's area. She was so excited for her friend. This was amazing news and it occurred to her that she hadn't even contacted her friend in the past several days. Of all the times when Mia needed a friend, Autumn had been too wrapped up in her own world lately and she was ashamed.

"Where's Mia?" she asked Jean, Ash's administrative assistant.

"She's in Ash's office."

Autumn rushed through the doors, eager to see her friend. It was also a convenient excuse to avoid Xander today, made better by the fact that it was true.

"I just heard the news!" she screamed and grabbed Mia into a huge hug. "I'm so relieved. I told you Ash could get you out of this mess!" she said, rocking back and forth with her arms around Mia's shoulders.

Mia laughed and tried to nod her head, but Autumn's grip was too tight. "You were right. He got everything all cleared up. I can't believe it's actually over!"

Autumn laughed, delighted. "We have to go out and celebrate!" she exclaimed. "Let's go do Durango's!"

"Yes!" Mia agreed, knowing that a margarita was exactly what she needed right now. "I'm totally in!"

They walked out, arm in arm, to the elevators, laughing and giggling as the relief over the past few weeks eked out of Mia's mind.

"Men!" a blond woman grumbled as she pressed the elevator call button over and over.

Mia smiled at the woman with genuine appreciation. "You're the woman who just helped me stay out of jail," Mia said. "Are you okay?"

Cricket Fairchild spun around and noticed the two lovely women behind her. "I'm sorry," she said and took a deep breath while closing her eyes. "Nothing a good martini can't fix," she said, trying to calm down. "Men are just so confusing!" she snapped, the calming breath obviously not working too well.

Mia knew the feeling. "Why don't you come with us? I don't know about the martinis," she cautioned, "but the margaritas at Durango's are perfect for anything that ails you."

"I'm not sure I should be around humanity right now," she came back.

Mia laughed. "That's exactly where I am. I'm Mia Paulson," she said. "And we're heading out to celebrate me not being in jail for the rest of my life."

Cricket smiled back, taking Mia's hand in hers. "That sounds like a perfect start to the weekend. I think I'll join you after all."

As they walked down the street to the bar, Autumn could feel the tension in her shoulders start to dissipate. It wouldn't completely go away, but at least she was out of the office and could avoid Xander for the rest of the day. If he found out she'd left, he would follow her and ask her what was going on. Right now, she couldn't handle a conversation with him. She was too vulnerable and too desperate to ignore the fact that her affair needed to be over with Xander. It had been so amazing, so wonderful and shockingly perfect. But she wasn't the kind of woman who could ignore other women in his life. Nor could she continue to delude herself that she could have an affair with a man who she knew would eventually move on to another woman.

Now that she knew the real man, she also knew that her love for him was stronger than she would like to admit.

She was in love with him. Plain and simple, she loved him with every particle of her being.

Unfortunately, she had to protect her self-esteem and leave before he broke her.

"Wait!" Mia exclaimed and Autumn blinked, about to drown her sorrows in the margarita. Turning around, she watched as Mia walked over to another table and spoke to a woman sitting alone. This was odd, Autumn thought. Mia was talking with one of the newest lawyers on Ash's team.

When the pretty woman came over and sat down with them, Autumn instantly knew that she was going to like this woman. Kiera Ward had a sadness in her eyes that indicated there was much more to her than just a dynamo criminal defense lawyer.

They laughed and drank margaritas, nibbled on the salty chips which just made them drink more. It was a vicious, ingenious cycle, Autumn thought as the conversation swirled around her. This was exactly what she needed. Women who were obviously in the same position she was in. Autumn listened and watched, noticing that Kiera had the same, sad look in her eyes that Autumn did, Mia was furious with Ash, which Autumn suspected was a defense mechanism for the feelings she was fighting and Cricket, the only blond at the table, was furious about something that was happening with Ryker.

The four women here were all victims of the Thorpe brothers' charm. Was there any way to avoid their power? It was shocking that four intelligent, strong women could fall so hard for men who obviously were eager to avoid any kind of commitment.

Xander sat with his brothers at the bar, listening to the four stunningly gorgeous women tear up all of his brothers, himself included. The blond was cute, but really had it in for his oldest brother. Kiera was going on and on about what a ridiculous division Axel headed up and Mia was slamming down the drinks but that was probably okay since she'd just been freed from a murder charge. Embezzlement charges had been pending today, but the whole thing had been dismissed when Cricket, the cute blond, recognized the assumed murder victim. Hard to prosecute a person for murder when the man showed up for meetings designed to commit fraud! What an idiot, Xander thought.

And then his eyes moved over to Autumn. She'd left the office earlier this afternoon. Initially, he'd been worried, but when he'd heard that she'd just gone out to celebrate her best friend's freedom, he took it all in stride. Autumn deserved to get out and have fun. She'd been working extremely hard lately, trying to not let anything slide just in case someone discovered their relationship.

"Should we say something?" Axel asked, leaning back, not looking like he was in the mood to stop any of the conversation. Who would? It was too revealing! These four women were revealing all their deep, dark secrets about the men in their hearts.

"I say we send them another pitcher," Ash said with a chuckle as Mia told the other three women what an obnoxious, untrusting, cynical man he was.

Xander watched Autumn take a long sip of the margarita, his body on fire as he looked at her sexy neck. He loved that neck, he told himself.

"They're going to feel this in the morning," Ryker said with a chuckle.

Ash chuckled as well, pretending to be wounded. "It will be their punishment for all the mean things they're saying about us."

Axel rolled his eyes. "Speak for yourself," he punched his younger brother. "Those ladies might be evil when they're hung-over."

Xander couldn't handle looking at Autumn any longer. He had to have her in his arms. "I think it's time to crash this party. Don't you gentlemen?" he asked and placed his half-finished beer behind him on the bar.

He didn't wait for them to agree, wanting to feel Autumn's softness against him too intensely. "Time to go, love," he said into Autumn's ear.

She turned around, startled to see him so close. "I'm not going anywhere with you," she said and picked up her drink, taking a long swallow.

"Why not?" he asked, pushing her drink away as soon as she put it back down on the table.

"Because Mia, Cricket and Kiera don't go around dating other women all the time. They're nice and fun and we understand each other."

Xander looked at his brothers, all of them trying to figure out how to get the women out of the bar. Ash had the best approach. He simply picked Mia up in his arms and carried her out. He heard her saying something about Ash being an obnoxious brute, but then she put her head on his shoulder and sighed with what sounded like happiness.

He didn't think Autumn would be as amenable to that solution. "How about if we go back to my place and talk about it?"

She snorted and shook her head. "No."

"Why not?" he asked, pulling her chair back and considering the best way to lift her into his arms.

"Don't even think about it," Autumn snapped at him. "Why don't you go find one of those women you've messed around with over the past few months?"

Ryker snorted at that comment. "He wishes!"

Xander glared at his older brother, not wanting his celibacy over the past...who knows how long...to become common knowledge.

Autumn picked up on the statement anyway. "What does he mean by that?" she asked.

"Nothing, love. Let's go."

"No. Because you're going to try and take my clothes off as soon as we get out of here."

He ignored his other brothers' laughter at her comment. "Yes, I am," he confirmed, taking her hands and pulling her up and into his arms. "Any objections?"

She pulled away and slung her purse over her shoulder. "Many."

She walked out of the bar, surprised at how steady on her feet she was after all those drinks. She was proud of herself for how well she'd handled her alcohol. A very responsible adult, she thought with pride.

Xander pulled two chairs out of her way before she crashed into them, then steered her out of the way of one of the tables. She looked pretty cute trying to pretend like she wasn't drunk, he thought. He wasn't going to let her even try to drive home though.

Out on the street, she looked to the right and left, trying to look for a cab so she could get home. She spun around, almost falling onto Xander in the process. "I forgot to pay our bar tab!" she gasped.

"Ryker took care of it," he reassured her, running his hands over her back.

He heard something to his left and almost groaned out loud when he heard Suzy Martin screeching as she looked at him. Suzy was a woman who had tried very hard to entice him into her bed about three months ago. She had long, blond hair, a body that was as thin and flat as a cracker and beautiful eyes.

"I thought you were gay!" she said at the top of her lungs!

Xander's eyes widened and he had to stop himself from laughing out loud. "Um, hello Suzy. How have you been?" he asked, extending his hand awkwardly. He wasn't immune to the hilarity of her comment either.

"Don't you dare ask me how I've been you bastard! You're supposed to be gay!"

He didn't roll his eyes, but it was close. "Why was I supposed to be gay?"

She flung her hands onto her barely-there hips, her cheekbones almost bursting out of her face because of a lack of body fat. "Because you weren't interested! In anyone!" she yelled back at him, obviously furious with him.

He smothered his amusement as the woman he was painfully interested in snuggled against his chest. "I've really got to go," he said, unconcerned with Suzy's opinion of his sexuality.

"What does she mean?" Autumn asked, sighing as she laid her head onto his shoulder. She knew she shouldn't, but he just felt so darn good!

"Don't worry about her," Xander said, leading her back to the parking garage and then gently tucking her into his car.

She was almost instantly asleep and he drove them straight to his place, not even considering heading back to hers. She'd said some strange things and he wanted her here where he could make sure to talk to her in the morning.

CHAPTER 9

Autumn reared up in bed, looking around and then groaned in pain as her head felt like it was going to split apart from the pain shooting across her forehead.

"You're not gay," she whispered.

Xander sat up as well and watched with concern as she worked through the discovery of her hangover. "No. I thought that was pretty clear."

She gripped her head in both hands while still trying to hold the sheet up over her body. "But Suzy said you weren't interested in anyone."

He got up out of bed and went into his bathroom. A moment later, he handed her a glass of water and some aspirin. "I wasn't interested in those women."

She took the aspirin and drank the entire glass of water. "Why weren't you interested in them? And why did she think you were gay?"

She leaned back, unaware that it was onto his chest and not the pillows. All she knew was that she felt wonderfully safe and warm.

"I can't speak for all of the women in Suzy's mind, but as for her, I wouldn't sleep with her. She wasn't happy about that."

Something in the back of her mind niggled at her memory. "What about that horrid woman yesterday?"

He rubbed her shoulders gently, trying to ease the pain of the hangover away but he suspected, from past, personal experience, that only time would ease her pain. "Which horrid woman are we discussing now?"

"The black-haired evil one that came in yesterday morning to speak with you."

His fingers stilled on her shoulders while he went through the people he'd had meetings with yesterday. "Are we discussing Marcy Duprey, by any chance?" he asked.

"I think that was her name." She leaned back, feeling slightly better now that the aspirin was starting to metabolize in her body.

Xander sighed. "Marcy Duprey came in to get her third prenuptial agreement signed. Her husbands have required it in the past."

That was definitely news to her. "Why?"

"Because she's a heartless, merciless woman who goes through husbands like other women go through stockings."

Autumn laughed slightly but then stopped when the pain in her head throbbed. "I think I drank too much last night," she sighed, rubbing her temples gently.

Something else occurred to her and she froze. Pulling away from him, she looked up into his eyes, needing to understand him. "What did your brother say last night?"

Xander rolled his eyes. "Which one? And at what time? They were saying a lot, probably a lot of things you didn't hear."

She shook her head then stopped when it hurt too much. "No, I heard this. It didn't make sense at the time."

Xander stiffened, worried about whatever his brothers might have said that would hurt her feelings. "Which comment, love."

She bit her lip, trying to think through the pain that was still throbbing. "Ryker said 'You wish' after I said something about you dating all those other women."

Xander pulled her back against his chest and resumed his massage. "Ryker doesn't know what he's talking about."

She heard the words, but something about the tone of his voice didn't ring true. "What aren't you telling me, Xander?" she asked, more worried now than she had been last night. "I don't understand you and I'd like to. But I can tell that you're hiding something."

Xander leaned his head back against the headboard slightly. "Are you sure you really want to do this?"

She thought about it for a long moment. "Yes. I think I do. Are you going to tell me something horrible? Like you're a secret serial killer and I'm your next victim? If so, maybe you really should keep that to yourself. If I'm going to die a horrible death, I'd rather not know about it in advance."

Xander was already laughing before she finished her comment. "No, I'm not a serial killer. But then, nor am I a serial dater."

"What's that supposed to mean?"

Xander moved his hands lower, easing the tension along her shoulder blades. "Are you sure you want to discuss this? It's going to change everything and you might not like what you hear."

And instantly, all the tension was right back with her. She pulled away from him and stood up, grabbing his shirt from the chair and buttoning it up before she turned around to face him. "Okay. Tell me. What's going on? What is this big secret?"

Xander leaned back against the headboard again, staring up at the ceiling. "I'm in love with you. My brothers have known about it for years."

She stood there, staring. Not understanding. "But all those women…"

"They were just a smoke screen."

She felt a small little flutter in her stomach. "So when that woman on the street said you were gay, it was because….?" She wasn't sure how to say it.

He ran a hand through his hair in frustration. "Suzy doesn't count."

That was a startling comment. "Why doesn't she count?"

"Because she's too thin. I wasn't even remotely attracted to her."

"And Jessica?"

Xander shrugged again. "Too aggressive."

"Marcy?"

He grinned. "Too mercenary."

She couldn't help but chuckle at that one. "And all the other women?"

His eyes turned wary and he hesitated. But when he saw the vulnerability in her eyes, he sighed and told her the truth. "They weren't you."

She gasped and tried to take another breath, but his words made her heart ache. In a good way this time. "How do I know?" she whispered.

He shook his head. "I can't prove anything to you. My brothers know I haven't slept with anyone for years. Suzy knows which is why she and all of her friends think I'm gay. I wouldn't sleep with any of them, no matter how much they tried to tempt me."

"You weren't tempted?"

"Not even in the slightest."

"But they're all beautiful," she stated as if he were crazy.

"They weren't you, Autumn."

She paced back and forth at the bottom of his bed, ignoring the pain in her head. "This doesn't make any sense. You're a very sexual man."

"I am with you. With other women, they leave me cold."

"We fight all the time!" she said, throwing her hands up in the air with exasperation.

"I like fighting with you," he grinned. "I like fighting and talking and laughing and cooking but most of all, I like making love to you. I love hearing your moans when I do something that you like."

She blushed and looked at her hands. "I moan all the time."

He laughed, nodding his head. "I know that. I like it."

She sat down at the end of the bed, her mind quickly moving through everything he'd told her this morning. "Why?" she asked, trying very hard to understand and believe what he was saying, but it was too hard. Because if he changed his mind, it would break her heart.

"Xander, are you trying to tell me that you haven't had sex with anyone since you met me?"

He shook his head. "No. I can't claim that. I've been with other women in that time. You were too young initially. And then you started dating that ass, Tim or Tom or something like that."

"Tim," she confirmed. "He was a nice guy."

"He was an ass. He had a wimpy handshake and he was afraid of spiders."

She laughed, remembering her telling her co-workers about how he'd jumped up on the kitchen chair when a spider had appeared in his kitchen one night. She'd had to kill it for him and left almost immediately afterwards. "You heard that conversation?" she asked.

"Yes. And went out and killed five spiders that day, just to prove my worth to you."

She laughed hard, even able to picture him going into the woods to find spiders. "You never told me about your killing spree."

He crossed his arms over his bare chest, denying her the view she liked so much.

She bit her lip, trying to figure out if she believed him or not. "So why haven't you said anything in all these years?"

"Because you didn't seem interested in me."

"We used to be friends."

"I want more than a friendship."

And here it was, she thought. This was the brass ring. Dare she ask the question? "What do you want?"

"You," he said without hesitation. "I want you in my home. In my bed. I want you to marry me and make me the happiest man in the world. I want to fight with you and make love to you ten times a day."

Her eyes widened. "Ten times?" she asked, shuddering.

"I have a lot of years to make up for," he explained. He waited tensely for her to respond to the other things he'd said but when she just sat there staring at her hands, he couldn't wait any longer. "Is there any way you might learn to love me?"

She laughed and hiccupped at the same time. "Xander, I've been in love with you ever since you bought me those leather, cashmere gloves after I lost mine."

His face was blank as he said, "Someone dropped them in the parking lot that day."

She crawled up the bed, knowing he was looking down the neckline of the shirt, staring at her breasts. "You bought them at the store around the corner an hour before you gave them to me. The salesclerk had the receipt delivered over to you since you forgot to pick it up before you left."

He grimaced, but since she'd reached him by this point, he helped her by lifting her up and arranging her so she was straddling him, exactly how he wanted her. "So I lied about that. What about the rest of what I told you?" he asked, his hands resting on her thighs.

She tilted her head to the side, considering all that he'd said. "I believe you." She grinned. "Or more specifically, I believe Ryker and Suzy."

Xander froze for a moment, then with a growl, he tossed her onto her back, tickling her in all the places he'd discovered she was ticklish. He didn't let up until she was begging him to stop, laughing so hard she could barely get the words out.

"I love you," he told her tenderly, kissing her smiling lips and looking down at her with all the love in his eyes.

Her fingers reached up to touch his hair and his face. "I love you too. I'm sorry it's taken us so long to realize it," she whispered.

He grinned lasciviously. "That's okay. I'll just have to make up for all the years you were too stubborn to realize what was going on," he said. And he started doing just that.

CHAPTER 10

"Is this your way of ensuring that I don't look at another woman?" Xander asked, leaning against the doorway to their bedroom.

Autumn swung around, her shocked eyes taking in his buff body in the tailored tuxedo. "Goodness," she breathed softly, unable to stop gawking. "Don't do that."

One eyebrow went up in inquiry. "Don't do what?"

"Wear that tuxedo. It's not legal."

He chuckled and walked into the bedroom where she was finishing up. "What's illegal is you, in this dress. I don't think I like seeing you in this dress."

She laughed and smacked his hands away but he ignored her efforts, just like she knew he would. She had just pulled on the blue, satin bridesmaid's dress for Mia's wedding. It was beautiful and sexy and she loved Xander's reaction so she didn't fight his hands too diligently. As if she would ever object to having his hands touch her in any way. "We're going to be late if you don't stop," she said as he bent lower and nibbled along her neck.

"I think I need some handcuffs," he said.

She laughed softly, but the idea had merit. "Who would be wearing the cuffs?"

"You, of course."

Shaking her head, she stepped out of his arms and slipped her shoes on, feeling better now that she didn't feel so short. In her heels, the top of her head at least reached his chin. "There's no 'of course' about it," she argued. "I don't think I should have to wear handcuffs after last night."

He grabbed her wrists and held her in place, just like he'd done the previous evening. "Ah, but you didn't learn your lesson well enough."

"I didn't know there was a lesson to learn."

"There's always something to learn," he came back, lifting her hand so that he could look at the diamond ring sitting there. His finger rubbed over the diamond and he smiled. "We're still not going to announce our engagement today?"

"Absolutely not. This is Mia's day."

He rolled his eyes. "And you think Mia didn't plan all of this?" he asked, indicating the satin blue dress she was wearing which was low cut and sexy as hell. "She's up to something and you know it."

Autumn laughed, agreeing with him. But since she and Xander were already a couple, neither of them minded that Mia was doing a little matchmaking. "So when are we going to announce our wedding?"

Xander shrugged. "Why announce it at all? Why don't we just fly out to Vegas and get married tomorrow?"

She thought about that for a moment, then nodded her head. "Okay."

He pulled her into his arms. "Would you really want to do that? What about a big wedding? Don't you want all of your friends there with you?"

She smiled slightly. "Well, Mia will be on her honeymoon, I can't invite Kiera and Cricket because they're sick of weddings after this one. And I don't want to wait another year or two for them to recover. So why don't we just have a small party when we get back?"

He thought about that for a moment, then shook his head. "No. I want my brothers there with me when I get married. And I want you to have your friends there. I know you've known Mia, Cricket and Kiera for only a few weeks, but the three of you seem like sisters already. They should be there, ready or not."

"We just finished helping Mia. I really don't want to go through all of this again."

He looked at her carefully. "Are you sure? You don't want the white dress and the flowers and all that stuff?"

She grinned. "I can still wear the white dress in Las Vegas. I don't need the flowers or the big reception. I just need you," she said and stretched up to kiss him.

Xander pulled her closer, deepening the kiss even while his mind was working out a plan. He wanted Autumn to have everything, so everything she will get.

MIA AND ASH'S WEDDING

"Do I look okay?" Mia asked nervously, smoothing down the yards of tulle that made up the skirt of her dress. "I probably shouldn't have…"

"You should have," Autumn soothed, pressing a gentle hand to Mia's shoulders while their eyes connected in the mirror. "You look stunning and Ash is going to be so happy when he sees you that he'll be speechless."

Kiera snorted and shook her head. "Ash is never speechless," she came right back, standing behind Mia as well. The sexy blue satin dress was still a shock whenever she looked in the mirror, but at least Axel knew what to expect. She'd dressed at Axel's house and had almost become undressed as soon as she'd walked out of the closet. He'd liked the dress very much.

Autumn and Cricket both laughed at Kiera's comment but Mia was too nervous to see the humor. "He spent too much money doing all of this," she said out loud.

Cricket moved to stand in front of her friend, a stern look on her face. "Mia, you've got to listen carefully. All combined, those Thorpe brothers have more money than a small country so I don't want to hear another word about how much all of this is costing. Ash wouldn't have spent so much trying to hurry this wedding along if he didn't want you to be his wife very much. So here's what's going to happen," Cricket explained with absolute determination. "You're going to go out there and see your man. You're going to forget all about the expense of this entire affair and you're going to have the best day of your entire life. All of your neighbors are out there, your friends, coworkers and a man who loves you so much that he's chomping at the bit to get you next to him. This is your day. Today you are the fairy princess and you're going to have the time of your life. Anything less and I will sneak into your house and do something really crazy and you won't even know I was there until you realize something strange is happening. Do we understand each other?"

Mia's eyes were wide throughout the whole speech until the end. When Cricket came up with that ambiguous threat, all three women laughed outright. "No you're not. You made a promise to Ryker that you wouldn't ever sneak into anyone else's house."

"Well, except for the businesses and houses that she's paid to sneak into," Kiera teased.

"Yes, except for those," Cricket smiled right back. "I really do have the best job in the entire world." Cricket was hired by Hamilton Securities to join an elite team of ex-military and intelligence personnel who traveled all over the world, testing the security of their clients' buildings and computers. And she was loving every moment of her new job.

Autumn shivered. "I would faint at the first sign of danger," she said, shaking her head at Cricket's crazy skills. "But I'm thrilled that you're happy now."

"Let's get this show on the road," Kiera interrupted. "But Autumn and I are with Cricket, my friend," she said to Cricket, giving her a gentle hug. "We'll be watching. Just so you know, we all have a pact to watch you. The first sign of worry and we're filling up your champagne glass. If you don't take our advice and enjoy today, we'll make sure you're too drunk to remember your stress. Got it?"

Mia laughed but nodded her head. "Got it," she told the three of them. They gave her a big, group hug, then leaned back, all of them checking their mascara in the mirror.

"Okay, let's go find my man," Mia said, tugging her strapless wedding gown slightly higher on her body. "By the way," she said to Cricket, "don't think I didn't notice that huge rock on your finger." She turned and fluffed her dress. "I actually noticed one on everyone's finger. So we're going to have a long chat when I get back from wherever Ash is taking me on our honeymoon."

The three other women looked at each other, then down at each person's left hand. Sure enough, there was a gorgeous diamond ring on each woman's finger.

"I guess I didn't need to go so crazy on those bridesmaids dresses after all," she said. Then she pulled her veil over her head, picked up her bouquet, and headed out of the anteroom of the church.

Autumn, Cricket and Kiera all looked at each other with stunned surprise for a long moment. Then burst out laughing. They looked around at each other, grabbed their own bouquet of flowers, and continued their almost hysterical laughter as they made their way out of the room to take their places at the back of the church.

Ryker, Ash, Axel and Xander all looked at each other when they heard the loud laughing as they stood at the front of the church waiting for the ceremony to start. When neither of them could figure out what was so funny on such a momentous day, they shrugged and looked at the minister who had a very disapproving expression on his face.

Ash didn't care what the minister thought, as long as he performed the ceremony that would make Mia his.

The music started and the laughing stopped. Behind him, he felt each of his brothers stiffen as the women in their lives entered the sanctuary but he couldn't think about them at all, too eager to see Mia.

When she finally appeared, he thought he might have died and gone to heaven. She looked so beautiful in the strapless gown that flared out all around her. She looked delicate, sexy and ethereal all at the same time. No woman had ever affected him like this little lady did. And he couldn't wait to make her legally his own.

She moved into place beside him and he moved her veil out of the way, his breath catching in his throat when she smiled up at him. "You're beautiful," he growled.

Ash wasn't sure what happened during the ceremony because his whole mind was focused on the last few words. "I now pronounce you husband and wife," the minister said with a smile that was warm and approving.

Ash turned to Mia, pulling her close and not even waiting for permission before he pulled her into his arms and kissed her thoroughly.

As they walked out of the church, Ash almost laughed at her trembling response. When they were in the waiting limousine, he pulled her onto his lap, his strong hands encircling her waist as he bent his head and kissed her again, just to feel her response which never failed to drive him crazy with lust for her. When he raised his head and looked down at her, he almost chuckled at the dazed expression on her lovely face. "You're mine now," he said.

Mia grinned and wrapped her arms around his neck more securely. "And you're mine," she whispered back.

Several hours later, Mia was exhausted. She hadn't left Ash's side all night. They'd danced, laughed with family and friends, ate tons of food and drank several glasses of champagne. But now, all she wanted was to be alone with her man, to have him wrap her in his arms and carry her away to some place private and quiet.

"Ready to go?" Ash asked when he felt her lean more heavily against his side. He'd been waiting for her to get her fill of the party before he took her away, but he was growing impatient to have her alone.

"More than ready," she said, smiling up into his blue eyes that she loved so much.

"Let's get out of here," he growled and pulled her closer. He was practically carrying her out of the reception area, wanting her in the car where he could slip that amazing dress off of her lovely figure and have his wicked way with her. "I want you alone."

"Not so fast," Ryker said, stepping in front of his youngest brother.

Ash halted, but only because it was his brother. Anyone else would be mowed down. When Xander and Axel stepped up, shoulder to shoulder with Ryker, Ash knew that he was going to have to fight his way out of this party. "Guys, you're my brothers and I love all of you, but that doesn't mean I won't take you down if you don't get out of my way pretty quickly.

His brothers just laughed, none of them worried about the threat. "We just wanted to say goodbye." Which was an outright lie. The ladies in their group had seen that the couple was trying to slip away unnoticed and had tasked the brothers to slow down the newly married couple so the rest of the guests could get organized.

"Not funny, guys," Ash growled.

When Xander heard the whistle, he gave the signal that everything was set up now. "We'll let you go now. But we'll see you back here in ten days. Lots of things happening."

Ash didn't care what was going on. All he wanted was to get Mia alone. "Clear the way," he told them firmly.

The brothers just smiled and stepped back, causing Ash to look at the three of them suspiciously. He put an arm around Mia's slender waist protectively, then pulled her along behind him.

As soon as they stepped out of the ballroom, a flurry of rose petals was thrown into the air, descending on the couple with delicate kisses of good luck. Mia glanced up, surprised at the shower of rose petals but enchanted nonetheless. She looked over at the three women dressed in similar blue satin outfits, her eyes clouding from the tears that were forming at the touching gesture.

Ash saw the look and stopped, letting Mia enjoy the flower rainfall, enchanted when several of the rose petals fell into her hair, balancing there precariously before falling to the ground.

"I don't think I've told you I love you," he whispered into her ear.

She grinned up into his eyes. "Every time you look at me," she whispered right back to him.

A moment later, they were driving away, Mia unaware of anything but Ash's arms around her, his lips kissing hers and the gentle sway of the limousine as it carried them towards the airport.

KIERA AND AXEL'S WEDDING

"I can't believe this is happening," she whispered. Her hand fluttered around the jeweled waist of her bodice. "Is this really happening?"

Autumn laughed and hugged her friend. "It's been a long time coming, but yes. You are finally marrying Axel."

"Six years!" she whispered. "Six long, miserable, lonely years." She almost started crying as she thought about how much time she'd missed with Axel. "I could have lost him."

Cricket stepped up and took Kiera's hand. "But you didn't. Which only means that this was meant to happen."

"Even the weather agreed with you!" Autumn said with a huge grin on her face.

Kiera shook her head. "I doubt there's going to be another day like today. I can't believe the sun is shining and it is so warm out in November!"

"Axel wanted you to have this wedding," Mia said, handing Kiera the bouquet of daisies and pink chrysanthemums. "And it is pretty spectacular!"

"It will get cold tonight," Kiera warned.

The three women waved away the warning. "Axel has those heaters stationed all around the dance floor under the pergola. We'll be toasty warm. Don't worry about a thing."

Kiera smoothed her hand down her dress one more time. "I don't think I could worry about anything anyway. I'm too excited."

Mia hugged her friend, feeling very relaxed and smug after returning from her honeymoon just the previous day. "It seems like the entire office building has shown up for your wedding. So go on out there and make us proud, girl!"

Kiera's smile widened even more. "You're right. Let's go do this!"

The enormous oak tree behind Axel's house was filled with pink lights, rows of pink chairs were lined up, filled with friends and co-workers, daisies were everywhere and the four Thorpe brothers were once again lined up, but with Axel at the front of the line this time.

When the bridesmaids stepped around the corner of his house, Axel craned his neck to get his first glimpse of Kiera. He even liked the dresses each of the ladies chose, thinking that they looked very pretty in the various shades of green.

But it was Kiera who caught his eye when she stepped around the corner. He'd pictured her so often in his house as he'd built it, refining it over the years but nothing could have prepared him for the sight of her in the blush pink, strapless wedding dress. She was stunning and the most beautiful woman he'd ever seen in his life.

She didn't wear a veil but stepped down the grassy aisle, walking towards him with tears in her eyes. "Are you okay?" he asked when she stepped closer and he could take her hands.

She gave him a watery smile, squeezing his hands as she said, "I cost us six years because of my stupidity. I'll make it up to you."

He almost laughed, delighted that she was still okay. "I thought you were starting to regret not accepting the job in Paris."

"Never. I only regret that we didn't do this the first time you suggested it."

He bent down and kissed her gently. "We have years ahead of us," he whispered. "Don't regret the past. It only diminishes the beauty of our future."

She thought that was the most profound thing she'd ever heard and moved closer to him, resting her head against his shoulder as she turned to face the minister. And when he finally pronounced them husband and wife, she thought her heart might just burst out of her chest with the love she felt for this man.

"You're wonderful," he said as he lifted her into his arms, swinging her around on the dance floor as the music started to play. For the rest of the night, they danced in each other's arms, barely noticing the rest of the guests. She didn't each much, wanting to be with him instead.

But Axel noticed that she wasn't eating anything and stacked food onto a plate from the buffet table that had been set up near his vegetable garden. "Here. You're going to have to eat something."

"I'm not hungry," she said and started to pull him into her arms for another dance.

He shook his head and pushed the plate towards her. "You're going to eat," he said and fed her some sort of appetizer that looked like shrimp and scallops somehow meshed together. "You're going to need your strength for the night ahead."

Kiera blushed, but she opened her mouth to taste the morsel. She ate several more of the delicious appetizers but by the time she'd had enough, she didn't remember anything she'd eaten.

When the party was winding down, Axel was too impatient to deal with the goodbyes. He remembered Ash's wedding and wasn't going to be hindered by his brothers while he tried to make his escape. So instead of announcing his departure, he simply lifted Kiera up into his arms and swept her out of the party. It took the guests another ten minutes before they realized that the bride and groom had already left but they continued dancing on into the night.

Kiera laughed, delighted at his exit strategy and threw her arms around his neck, more than willing to be kidnapped out of her own party.

CRICKET AND RYKER'S WEDDING

"Where are we going?" Cricket asked, taking Ryker's hand but hesitant. He had one of those expressions on his face that told her he was up to no good.

"Do you trust me?"

She laughed and shook her head. "Not when you're looking like that."

His rumbling laughter made her feel all warm and gushy inside. "Well, you're going to have to."

She closed the door on her tiny house for the last time, looking at him carefully. "Why won't you tell me what's going on?" she demanded, pulling her scarf closer around her as the freezing wind whipped around the corner of her house. It had been three weeks since Kiera's wedding and, as predicted, the weather had turned painfully cold, the usual for Chicago's winters.

He shook his head. "You're going to have to trust me."

She laughed and let him tuck her into his car. "I would, if you would give me more information."

He shrugged. "Let's just say I'm taking things into my own hands," he told her and slammed the door shut on her confused expression.

When he was seated next to her, she glared at him. "What are you doing, Ryker?" she demanded more forcefully.

He didn't answer her and she started to become concerned when he drove to the airport. She almost groaned when she saw O'Hare in the distance. "Another job? But I thought I had a few weeks off after the last project," she said. "I'm going to talk to Mitch. He told me he had nothing on the horizon for the next two weeks. I've been working non-stop trying to get things organized…"

"Relax," Ryker said as he drove through the lanes, pulling up into the private parking area of the airport. "This trip is just for you and me."

She liked the sound of that! "Well, if you insist."

"I insist."

She stepped out, slipping her hands into her gloves and pulling her hat down lower over her head. "This is miserable," she grumbled.

"You've been taking too long to organize our wedding," he told her as he led her out of the parking area and straight onto the tarmac where The Thorpe Group's private jet was standing by.

Cricket sighed and hugged his arm. "I'm sorry. I know it's taking too long. I just…"

He stopped and looked down at her. "You don't want to get married in the winter," he said, his eyes understanding.

She smiled, relieved that he understood. "Not really. I don't like the cold and I was hoping for an outdoor wedding. I loved the way Kiera's wedding felt and wanted the same thing."

He smiled and winked down at her. "Come on," he said and squeezed her fingers. "I have a trip to make. You have some time off so you're coming with me. You'll relax, I'll get my mission accomplished and we'll have some time together."

Cricket didn't hesitate. She followed him up the stairs and was relieved when they were able to sit down in the large, comfortable leather chairs. She picked up a magazine while Ryker conferred with the pilot. Ten minutes later, the jet was taxiing down the runway and Cricket fell asleep with her head snuggled against Ryker's shoulder. She fell asleep listening to the soothing sounds of his deep voice next to her and loved it.

She had no idea what time it was when she felt his strong hand shake her shoulder slightly. "Cricket. It's time," he said.

She sat up slowly, looking around to get her bearings. "Goodness," she gasped, releasing her tight hold on his arm as she woke up and took in her surroundings. "Where are we?" she asked.

"Grand Cayman," he told her with a chuckle at her bewildered expression. "You need to change your clothes."

She looked at him as if he'd lost his mind. "Why? Can't I change at the hotel? Or wherever we're staying?"

He shook his head. "Nope. There won't be time."

That was a strange thing to say. "Okay. But what's going on?"

He took her hands and looked down into her eyes. "We're getting married today, love," he said firmly.

She blinked, still not accepting what he was telling her. "Why would we do that?"

He squeezed her fingers slightly. "Your dress is in the bedroom behind you," he explained. "Your friends are already here and we're getting married."

She almost laughed at his expression. "What's the temperature?" she asked, moving closer to him, snuggling up to his big, broad chest.

"It is a balmy eighty degrees."

Her smile widened at the idea. "Mia, Autumn and Kiera are here already?"

"Yes."

"And your brothers?"

"Yes. They all arrived yesterday."

She laughed, delighted with the idea. "You've been a busy boy, haven't you?"

He shrugged. "You're not angry?"

She leaned in and hugged him. "On the contrary. I'm thrilled! I wish I'd thought of this."

"Your parents are impatient to get the thing done with as well. Your mother was very helpful."

Cricket laughed again. "She's pretty good about planning parties. She loves to do it."

"Well, I basically gave her cart blanche but with several stipulations. It had to be in a warm climate and I wanted it done this weekend."

She grinned, thinking of the conversation between this strong-willed man and her mother who always got her way. "I guess I'd better get changed then."

She spun around on her heel, thrilled with the idea of getting married here on the island. When she stepped into the back room of the private plane, she saw her wedding dress already laid out along with the fabulous shoes she'd found last week. This couldn't have worked out better if she'd done all of this herself. But truth be told, she'd been so exhausted trying to move out of her house, put it on the market and work at her new job. She'd been frustrated that she hadn't made more progress on her wedding plans but knew that she'd been procrastinating because she'd wanted a summer wedding. Now she was going to get one!

When she stepped off of the plane, an official looking gentleman was standing at the bottom of the stairs right next to her father and mother. "Ready to get married?" he father asked, taking her into his arms and hugging her gently.

"Very ready," she whispered excitedly.

Her mother laughed and hugged her as well. "I think you're going to be pleasantly surprised."

"Ryker said you'd organized all of this?" she prompted, trying to find out details.

But her mother knew exactly what Cricket was trying to do and she wasn't going to wheedle any details. "I organized it all, but Ryker gave me very specific details about what he wanted. So don't let him fool you. He is the mastermind of this fabulous gala. We just set the pieces in motion."

And that was the only information she was going to get. They helped her into the waiting limousine and off they went. When she stepped out of the limousine on her father's arm, she gasped in surprise. The sun was setting over the ocean and her friends were all standing in a casual grouping right in front of a filmy canopy that had been constructed next to the ocean. The pathway was littered with red roses and lit by candle filled lanterns. And at the end of the romantic pathway, Ryker stood in a white linen jacket and slacks with a white shirt. His three brothers stood next to him in similar suits. And Mia, Kiera and Autumn were also standing there waiting, in flowered sundresses with their hair pulled up off of their necks and held there with flowers. All of them had been in on the surprise, and Cricket wasn't sure if she was going to burst into tears or laugh with delight. So she did both.

A quartet started to play music off to the side and Cricket's father took one of her hands while her mother took the other. They'd never been a traditional family before and she didn't want them to start now.

When Cricket stepped forward and took Ryker's hand, she couldn't stop the tears from falling. "This is beautiful," she whispered up to his handsome face. "I couldn't have planned anything so lovely myself."

"It's okay?" he asked gently, his strong hand cupping her face while his thumb rubbed the tears from her cheeks.

"It's more than okay. It's wonderful."

They turned at that point, and fifteen minutes later, they were husband and wife. Ryker kissed her so gently, deepening the kiss as the waves crashed against the sand. It wasn't until everyone laughed and Xander pounded Ryker on the shoulder that he finally lifted his head.

"Time to party," Xander said and reached over, grabbing Autumn's hand in his. "This way," he told everyone.

They were led over to a wooden patio that was surrounded by lush, green plants and huge, colorful flowers. There was a tropical buffet set up with music and dancing. Ryker had reserved the entire restaurant just for them and they danced, laughed and ate decadent foods with an elaborate chocolate bar for dessert. The cake was all white with delicate butterflies set on the edge, looking like they were about to flutter away. It was so lovely, Cricket almost didn't want to cut it but everyone encouraged her to go ahead and they feasted on lemon wedding cake.

When he took her hand to lead her out the door, he whispered, "I love you," into her ear.

Cricket smiled up into those amazing blue eyes of his, still surprised by how much she loved this man. "I love you too," she finally said, unable to hide the happiness since it was about to burst out of her at any moment. "You make me happier than I've ever been in my life."

He kissed her gently as he led her down the hallway to the suite he'd reserved for their honeymoon. "Ah, a challenge! I accept," he teased her.

AUTUMN AND XANDER'S WEDDING

Autumn zipped the strapless bodice up her side, then bit her lip in anticipation of sliding her feet into her jeweled shoes. She wasn't sure, but she might actually love her silver shoes more than she loved her lace, tea length wedding gown.

The four of them were standing in the enormous suite Xander had reserved for them, ensuring that the Las Vegas hotel was everything Autumn had dreamed it might be. There was champagne chilling for the four of them along with delicacies to nibble on while they prepared for the final Thorpe wedding.

"Oh my," Cricket whispered when Autumn took her wedding shoes out of the shoe box that had been lovingly protecting them for the past six weeks. "How many times have you tried these on?" she asked with reverence.

Autumn laughed and slid her toe into the slender strap that would hold her toes in place. "Every time Xander isn't at home with me," she said, her eyes closing with delight. She opened them up and snapped the chain around her ankle which would hold the shoe on her foot.

"So not very often," Kiera teased.

Autumn nodded her head. "Not often enough but I'd rather have him home with me than trying on these shoes."

"They're magnificent," Mia sighed. "But I don't know how you wear heels that high all the time."

Autumn laughed, having heard that often. "I love them. They make me feel stronger. And I need that when Xander's around."

Kiera's eyes widened at her friend's statement. "Still? I thought you wore them before because he intimidated you."

She nodded her head as she adjusted the delicate chain on the second foot. "I used to wear them because of him. Goodness, he used to irritate me!" she laughed

111

again. "Now I just wear them because he always makes me feel weak in the knees. These help me stand up to him."

Kiera rolled her eyes. "Like you do that very often."

Autumn grinned. "So he's a pussy cat now."

Cricket adjusted the pin in Autumn's hair slightly then stepped back. "I think it's time you married this pussy cat of yours."

Autumn stood up and surveyed her appearance in the mirror. "I would have to agree with you," she said with excitement shooting through her whole body.

"Are you ready?" Kiera asked.

The four women stood together, all smiling, all beautiful and three of them newly married. "Would you have believed that all of us would be married six months ago?" Autumn asked, truly amazed by the changes in the past few months.

"Never," Mia laughed. "Of course, I didn't think I would have been arrested either."

The four of them laughed because she'd met her husband the morning she'd been arrested for murdering her previous fiancé, who hadn't been murdered at all. He was, in fact, serving time in prison with his current fiancée for fraud and embezzlement.

"This is a truly astonishing moment," Cricket said, taking the hands of Kiera and Autumn. Autumn then grasped Mia's hand and the four of them stood in front of the large mirror, three of them in colorful bridesmaid's dresses and one in white lace wedding finery.

"Let's get this show on the road," Autumn whispered. "Otherwise, I'm likely to break into tears."

"That would be bad."

The four of them were about to move, but Autumn stopped them. "Wait," she called out and all four women stopped and stared. "I just wanted to say thank you to all of you. Mia and I might have known each other for years, but it feels like the four of us have been sisters forever. I couldn't have gotten through those miserable months without the support of you three. And I'm deeply touched that I was able to stand with each of you as you married the men you love. But more, I'm honored that you are here with me today, ready to witness my own wedding to Xander."

Mia, Kiera and Cricket all wiped their tears from their eyes quickly then laughed nervously before they melted into a group hug. "You guys are the best," Kiera said fervently.

"Come on, ladies," a deep voice said from the doorway of their suite. "You're going to be late and you know how irritated Xander gets when someone is late."

Autumn stood up and rolled her eyes. "He can just be irritated," she said to Axel who stood in the doorway trying to usher everyone out to the ceremony. But she also hurried out of the room, not looking back for anything. This was her day.

It felt like she'd waited so long for this moment to arrive and everything was so much more wonderful than she could have imagined.

Having gone through formal weddings with Mia and Kiera, then a beach wedding with Cricket, Autumn and Xander had agreed that the only way to get married was to do it in style. So they had flown everyone out to Las Vegas for an extravagant wedding at The Bellagio Hotel.

The wedding coordinator was standing outside their door, eager to escort them to the wedding area. When Autumn stepped into the Terrazza do Songo, she couldn't contain her gasp of surprise. It was like they were standing in the middle of a quaint, Italian village with flowers cascading everywhere. And as they looked out over the edge of the patio, the famous Bellagio fountains were dancing to an old Elvis song. She smiled at all the over-the-top details that Xander had arranged, feeling deeply touched.

The music started, swelling to a fabulous crescendo when Autumn stepped out. She walked down the short aisle, her eyes never leaving the tall, handsome man waiting for her at the end. When she stood beside him, she felt like she was floating on a cloud of happiness. And that was before he looked down at her shoes, then poked his own foot out. When she saw what he was silently pointing to, she burst out laughing.

Xander was wearing blue suede shoes!

"I love you, crazy man!" she whispered and leaned forward to kiss him even before the ceremony started.

"I love you to. And I love your shoes!"

It was nice to be marrying a man who knew how to make a woman feel special, she thought. Then they turned to the officiator, smiling as they listened to the beginning of the ceremony.

EPILOGUE

Five years later, Autumn waddled out of their bedroom and glared at Xander as he lifted their three year old daughter up into his arms. "Xander, what did you give Leandra for breakfast!" she demanded, but already knew the answer.

"What did we have for breakfast?" he asked Leandra who covered her mouth with her chubby hands to stifle her giggle.

"Nothing," she said carefully, then looked up at her father for his approval.

"Well, we had something," he corrected, winking at her.

"Oh!" she said and giggled again. "Milk and an apple, Momma," she recited just as she'd been prompted a moment ago.

"And chocolate cake?" Autumn asked, dumping sunscreen into their bag.

"Hello?" someone called out from the foyer.

Leandra instantly wiggled down from her father's arms, eagerly running to greet her cousin Jeremy who was two months older than she was, but still nice about it, she said every time the subject was brought up.

Mia walked in with Abby in her arms, dodging Leandra and Jeremy as they rushed by.

"Don't go out to the pool until an adult is with you!" she called out with a sigh. "Chocolate cake again for breakfast Xander?"

Xander's eyes widened. "How…?"

Ash walked in a moment later, shaking his head. "I'd never be able to get away with that," he said and bent down to kiss Autumn's cheek. "How are you feeling today? Any better?"

Autumn put one hand to the small of her back while the other covered her eight and a half month pregnant tummy. "I'd be better if my husband would stop feeding our daughter sugar for breakfast."

"She's fine," Xander countered and punched his younger brother on the arm before turning back to argue with his wife. "She needs a bit of chocolate every now and then to counter the tofu sausage you're always giving her. She needs a bit of fat." He patted his stomach where the six pack was even more defined than it had been on their wedding day five years ago.

There was more commotion from the side of the house, announcing the arrival of Ryker and Cricket along with their two year old twins, Kayla and Courtney. They constantly wanted to keep up with Jeremy and Leandra, both of whom encouraged the twins to run right alongside them.

As soon as Leandra ran through the kitchen, Cricket shook her head. "Chocolate cake again?"

Xander stared at his sister-in-law, astonished. "How does everyone know about the chocolate cake?" he asked. Unfortunately, he didn't get an answer since Axel and Kiera showed up with their son, Matthew, who immediately raced through the house in search of Leandra and Jeremy.

"You need to get off your feet," Axel said as he bent down to kiss Autumn's cheek, then stole Abby away from Mia, tickling Abby's tummy until she was laughing hysterically. "Why aren't you in the pool? Kiera loved the pool when she was pregnant with Matthew. Took all the pressure off of her back."

"I'm with you," Autumn said and pushed herself off of the chair. Xander was instantly right beside her, helping her up and holding her hand while they herded all the kids out to the pool area. There was a fence with a locked gate, just to make sure little feet didn't get near the pool without adult supervision and the little arm floaties already attached.

Autumn didn't stop in anyway as she lowered her very pregnant body into the pool, instantly feeling relief from the pressure in her back. Mia, Cricket and Kiera joined her, handing her a glass of icy lemonade as well. Xander plunked a wide-brimmed hat on her head, gave her a kiss, then moved off to supervise the kids in the shallow end.

"Goodness, why do men gravitate towards the grill?" Cricket asked as she watched her husband move off to fire up the grill in the corner of the pool area.

The others just smiled and laughed. Xander and Ash were in the pool, tossing kids around, plunking them on their shoulders and making sure they were all having a good time. Ryker was busy cooking their lunch while Axel gave Abby her bottle in the shade.

"Who would have thought," Kiera said out loud as she looked around at the chaos and happiness.

"Not me," Mia said with a smile.

"I'm glad it all worked out so well," Autumn said, sinking lower into the pool and sipping her lemonade.

"I think 'well' is putting it pretty mildly," Cricket said with a sigh of happiness. Ryker must have heard her because he turned in her direction and winked before re-focusing on the burgers and hot dogs.

"Are those tofu dogs?" Mia whispered.

"Yes," Autumn said, laughing at their secret. "I put them into the beef hot dog package so the guys wouldn't know."

The other women couldn't contain their laughter. Four men and five kids stopped what they were doing to survey the laughing women, grins on all of their faces before they turned back to what they had been doing.

"Yes, life is pretty good, even with tofu," Kiera said happily. And the other three nodded their heads in agreement.

EXCERPT FROM
THE BILLIONAIRE'S MASQUERADE,
BOOK 1 IN THE FRIENDSHIP SERIES

Rachel stepped out of her vehicle, surprised that the only irritation she felt was a bird's mild call in the distance. Where was the oppressive heat? Where was the humidity that caused a body to long for a cold, refreshing drink? Looking around, she took a deep breath and smelled nothing but….was that nature? She almost laughed, thinking of her childhood memories. As an adult, her morning smells were coffee, sometimes suffocating car exhaust and, depending on the day, the irritating scent of the photocopier ink when someone was printing out a large print job. It had been a long, long time since she'd smelled anything so…organic.

And the sounds! She stood absolutely still for a long moment. There was nothing but a bird calling out for her mate in the distance and a few rustling sounds as the wind played tag with the leaves on the trees.

If it weren't for her urgent, career-changing meeting, she might actually relax.

She suddenly realized what she was doing and shook her head, trying to clear her mind of both the memories as well as the idea that dirt could be a good smell. She hated dirt. She hated the heat of the summer sun pressing down on the top of her head until she felt like sinking to her knees in defeat. It wasn't that hot at the moment, but she suspected it could be. No, she preferred a nice, air conditioned room where she didn't feel her silk blouse sticking to her skin or the wall-like impact of the intense humidity of summers in Virginia.

Rachel tugged her black blazer down over her hips, smoothing out the expensive fabric in the hope that she didn't look as terrified as she felt.

"This is it," she whispered as she stood outside her little rental car, staring at the rough, gravel road ahead of her. "Why the man had to live out here in the middle of nowhere..." she left the end of the disparaging sentence dangling. Her prey was a recluse; no photos of Emerson Watson could be found and he was notoriously grouchy and mean. An ogre, according to some. So it was probably a good thing that the man lived out here all alone. No one to irritate him, he couldn't hurt other's feelings and he probably was able to concentrate better out here in the middle of nowhere...yes, grouchasaurs should be isolated.

She thought of the movie with the huge green man and the plaid, frayed pants. Keeping that silly image in her mind helped abate some of the anxiety over her unannounced interference in the man's obvious preference for isolation and solitude.

"But that's not going to stop me!" She started forward, almost tiptoeing down the dirt and gravel road so her three inch heels, her favorite red ones that made her feel strong and confident, wouldn't get dirty. "First impressions," she gritted out, wanting to make a good first impression with the man in question.

As she walked down the driveway, she ignored the low-level buzzing that was coming from the bushes, pretending to not be nervous about the possible bee hives that could be hidden in the tall, flowered shrubberies. Instead, she stared straight ahead, refusing to be intimidated by either the length of the driveway or the height of the bushes surrounding her. It almost felt like she was walking out of civilization. It seemed so isolated, almost lonely back here. Rachel wasn't the kind of person who needed people around at all times, but there was something almost...desolate about this gravel road. Why would anyone want a one lane road leading to their house? How could people easily come and go, socialize and network?

Okay, the man is famous for being a recluse. So he probably doesn't socialize. He is probably fat and gross and irritating so no one cared that he had a crazy-long, almost inaccessible driveway because they never visited!

She'd been walking for perhaps ten minutes when she heard a different, non-nature produced sound. It was very faint, but definitely a sound other than a bird or un-seen, rustling animal and her shoulders relaxed somewhat. At least there was some form of humanity out here along the rustic, Maine coastline!

She pulled on the bottom of her jacket one more time, assuming the only person who would dare to be out in this crazy nature stuff would be none other than the reclusive Emerson Watson himself. She smoothed the wisps of hair back that had escaped during her precarious trek and straightened her shoulders, trying to appear as tall and confident as possible.

Taking the last few steps around the latest bend in the driveway, she looked around with what she hoped was a gracious smile on her face. But as soon as she took in the sight, she slumped in frustration. This couldn't be Emerson Watson's house. The one bedroom cottage had all the windows open, a comfortable looking rocking chair on the front porch where several new boards needed to be replaced and weeds growing all over the cracked, concrete sidewalk. She could see the potential of the cottage. With some work, this tiny house could be very quaint and comfortable. She didn't know what it looked like inside, but the outside looked rundown and almost sad.

Nope, the shockingly wealthy Emerson Watson wouldn't be caught dead in this abode, she thought with disappointment. She looked to the left and the road continued further through even more bushes so this tiny little cottage must be someone else's home.

It was cute enough, she thought. Maybe some bright curtains on the windows, a few pillows and comfortable chairs on the front porch…some shrubs and flowers to soften the outside. Well, and a good coat of paint…yes, this house could be perfect!

But Emerson Watson was one of the ten wealthiest men in the world. He was a legend in the investment community with a reputation for being ruthless in business. The man had built up his investment corporation, luring the wealthiest clients from all over the world, and compounding their wealth several times over with his secretive investment strategies. The Securities and Exchange Commission investigated him five years ago as a possible Ponzi scheme because his investments almost never lost money and earned significantly higher than the average funds could even dream of achieving. He'd been completely exonerated and the investigation, which would leave some investors doubtful, had instead only added to the Watson legend.

Now Rachel wanted in. Emerson Watson chose one stock broker every year as an intern, teaching that person his secrets. Rachel wanted to be that person this year. She was sick of being one in a large ocean of stock brokers. Every intern Mr. Watson selected went on to gather even more clients. No one ever left his employ, simply moving from being an intern to an employee who worked out of whatever office in the world they chose.

She was determined to do everything in her power to become his next intern. She'd psyched herself up to not allow any of his reputed grouchiness to hurt her feelings. She was tough and impervious to insults. Well, in truth, Rachel admitted to herself that she might be a tad bit too sensitive, but she could learn to be hard and tough. She could learn anything. And Emerson Watson was the man who was going to teach her!

She was no longer playing it safe. She was going to get out into the world and push herself out of her comfort zone. Even this little weekend adventure to speak with the elusive Emerson Watson was hugely out of her comfort zone! She pretended that her knees weren't shaking with fear and her hands weren't trembling. This was how successful people became more successful!

She was intrepid!

Okay, so she wanted to be fearless. Just "fake it till you make it" was her new motto.

Turning around, she looked down the driveway, gearing herself up for another long hike, biting her lip in indecision. She looked down the gravel road, trying to calculate in her mind how far she'd walked already and how much further the main house might be. So she didn't see the movement to the left of her until it was almost too late.

Emerson Jackson Watson almost fell off of the ladder on which he was working when the woman emerged from the around the corner. Where the hell had she come from? He hadn't heard anything a moment ago and she'd just appeared with her sexy red shoes and full, luscious lips that she was nervously mauling with her pretty, white teeth.

He steadied himself and leaned his arm against the low roof of the cottage, his eyes taking in the strikingly beautiful mystery woman with the incredible legs and impossibly high heels teetering on her toes as she walked down the driveway. Her black suit cinched in at the waist, giving him a perfect view of her sexy figure. Did she have any idea how feminine she appeared? He suspected she'd chosen that black suit and those smoking hot, red shoes as a power play, but it had backfired because her breasts were too full, pressing against the black fabric of her suit jacket and her waist seemed tiny in comparison. Those heels only made her legs look like a stripper's although he suspected she'd paid four or five hundred dollars for those killer shoes.

His eyes traveled back up her figure, appreciating all the delicious, appealing details until his eyes reached her face and he couldn't stop the punch to his gut when he took in her full lips and almond shaped eyes surrounded by thick, black lashes. There was barely any gloss left to shine on those lips which only allowed her natural color to come through. And those pink, luscious lips were enticing enough but her eyes! Those green eyes were startling!

He wanted to stare into those eyes with the lengthy, thick lashes while he filled her up. He wanted to see what those eyes looked like when she was smiling or sad or, even better, when she was....

He shook his head and tried to remove those images from his mind. Women were a distraction he didn't need. When he needed a woman's touch, he had several lady friends in town who were more than accommodating. He definitely didn't need a wannabe power woman.

"Can I help you?" he asked, enjoying her surprise when she saw him.

Rachel's eyes snapped to the right and she couldn't stop the gasp that blew from her lungs when she looked over at the man standing on the ladder by the house. As an avid gym-goer, Rachel knew what a buff, male body looked like. And this man's physique was beyond anything she'd ever seen. She wasn't sure how tall he was since he was standing on a ladder, but she suspected that he was taller than the average man. But the extraordinary things were the rippling, amazing muscles that covered his body. It wasn't like he was a body builder with bulging muscles all over, but there were plenty of those. It was more that there were just muscles….everywhere! He was tall and lithe with those sumptuous, extraordinary muscles covering every part of his body. Her eyes did an inventory of all those muscles, irritated when she couldn't see past the low riding, well-worn jeans that were loose around his hips.

She swallowed painfully when those muscles flexed and she looked up, suddenly realizing that he was moving. Towards her! All those lovely, sweat-covered muscles were descending that ladder, his strong hands flexing as he grasped and un-grasped the ladder as he climbed down and her eyes were drawn to the appearing and disappearing muscles along his arms and back. Everything glistened in the sunshine and she felt like she was going to pass out from the blood rushing through her body at a crazy, pulse pounding rate.

That was when she realized that she'd stopped breathing and she took a gasping breath, trying to quickly regain her equilibrium. She was just starting to find her balance when she realized how tall he was. As he approached, she had to lean her head back farther and farther until he was standing about a foot away from her, towering over her with crystal blue eyes that were so startling, she thought she might just melt into a pool of lust right there on the gravel driveway.

When she realized she was just staring at that gorgeous expanse of tanned, muscled chest with her fingers and palms itching to touch all that glorious skin, she closed her eyes and shook her head. "I'm so sorry," she whispered, her embarrassment painful.

"What are you sorry for?" he asked softly, feeling cold now that her heated eyes weren't traveling up and down his body.

She didn't like the breathy sound of her voice, but she didn't like the way she'd objectified this stranger. She'd treated him abominably and she was ashamed. "I was looking at you inappropriately," she admitted, stiffening her shoulders and trying to look anywhere but at his chest. Didn't the man have a shirt?

His soft laughter melted over her tense shoulders until he said, "Don't worry about it. I was doing the same to you before you realized I was here."

She hmphed at that and looked at the house, at the beaten up old truck with all the painting equipment and tools piled in the back. She wasn't exactly sure how to react to that, but wished she hadn't blushed so brightly. "Well, still…."

"What brings you out to Cape Elizabeth?" he asked gently.

Rachel stared at her hands, then back at the cottage again. "I'm…um…" it took her several seconds to remember why she'd actually come here. She looked around…the bushes, the gravel drive, the cottage…none of it made sense with this gorgeous, muscled stranger standing in front of her. All her mind could think about, wonder about was how much she wanted to touch his skin, to taste him and bury her nose….

Good grief! She'd never reacted to a man like this before and she was horrified at her undisciplined behavior!

Focus! She wasn't here to gawk!

What was she doing here? And where was the man's shirt?! "Oh…I'm looking for someone," she answered, relieved when her memory returned. Was that piece of fabric draped over the bannister of the front porch his shirt?

She stepped around the extremely large male and walked over to the piece of fabric and picked it up, refusing to lift it to her nose to smell it. Surely it smelled awful, wouldn't it? But the man didn't smell. At least not bad. There was something….just right about the way he smelled despite the sweat covering all those fabulous, taut muscles.

She handed the shirt to him delicately, silently indicating he should put the shirt on and cover himself in front of her.

Unfortunately, the subtle hint didn't really work though because the obnoxious man just tossed that shirt over his shoulder. Rachel wasn't sure if she was irritated that he hadn't covered up some of those muscles or if she was relieved that he hadn't put the shirt on and covered all of them so she could speak with him intelligently. His exposed chest was making her stupid!

"Who are you looking for?" he asked, wiping his hands on a rag he dug out of the back of the truck.

"He's probably your employer," she said carefully, looking down to check her red shoes. "Mr. Emerson Watson."

"Why do you want to talk to him?" the stranger asked.

Why had he gone tense for that fraction of a second? He must not like his employer, Rachel sighed. If everything she'd heard about Mr. Watson was true, she wasn't going to enjoy working for him either.

She looked around, desperate to focus once more on her mission but she was having trouble with him standing there with his bare chest looking so enticing! "Could you please put that shirt on?" she snapped, glaring at him.

COMMENTS FROM THE AUTHOR

For some fun visuals on Xander and Autumn, go to:

http://www.pinterest.com/elennoxromances/his-challenging-lover/

If you have time, please take a moment to write a review on whichever platform you purchased this book. It not only helps guide others who might purchase this book, but I also love hearing from my readers – the good, the bad and the ugly. Some readers tell me there's too much sex, some tell me I should add more, others criticize my grammar and others tell me they love my books. Everything you write, I use to improve my next story. If you love what I write, let me know because I'll continue writing in the same way. If you think I should improve in some way, please let me know. I have a very tough skin and can take it – although I absolutely LOVE the positive reviews/comments.

If you would like to contact me directly, I can be reached at elizabeth@elizabethlennox.com. I try very hard to answer all e-mails because I love hearing from readers so much! It is a thrill to hear from you. But I apologize in advance if I miss responding to your message. Sometimes, things get lost in the inbox. I'm one of those non-techy people so I don't always see things that others might think are obvious. It isn't a slight – I promise. It is just that my mind is off in romance-world and not in the techy-world (much more fun/interesting/exciting in my romance-world even though my husband bangs his head against the desk sometimes when I don't understand the techy-world).

BOOKS BY ELIZABETH LENNOX

The Texas Tycoon's Temptation

The Royal Cordova Trilogy
Escaping a Royal Wedding
The Man's Outrageous Demands
Mistress to the Prince

The Attracelli Family Series
Never Dare A Tycoon
Falling For The Boss
Risky Negotiations
Proposal To Love
Love's Not Terrifying
Romantic Acquisition

The Billionaire's Terms: Prison Or Passion
The Sheik's Love Child
The Sheik's Unfinished Business
The Greek Tycoon's Lover
The Sheik's Sensuous Trap
The Greek's Baby Bargain
The Italian's Bedroom Deal
The Billionaire's Gamble
The Tycoon's Seduction Plan
The Sheik's Rebellious Mistress
The Sheik's Missing Bride
Blackmailed By The Billionaire
The Billionaire's Runaway Bride
The Billionaire's Elusive Lover
The Intimate, Intricate Rescue

The Sisterhood Trilogy
The Sheik's Virgin Lover
The Billionaire's Impulsive Lover
The Russian's Tender Lover
The Billionaire's Gentle Rescue

The Tycoon's Toddler Surprise
The Tycoon's Tender Triumph
The Sheik's Mysterious Mistress
The Duke's Willful Wife
The Sheik's Secret Twins

The Tycoon's Marriage Exchange
The Russian's Furious Fiancée
The Tycoon's Misunderstood Bride

Love By Accident Series
The Sheik's Pregnant Lover
The Sheik's Furious Bride
The Duke's Runaway Princess

The Russian's Pregnant Mistress

The Lovers Exchange Series
The Earl's Outrageous Lover
The Tycoon's Resistant Lover

The Sheik's Reluctant Lover
The Spanish Tycoon's Temptress

The Berutelli Escape
Resisting The Tycoon's Seduction
The Billionaire's Secretive Enchantress

The Big Apple Brotherhood
The Billionaire's Pregnant Lover
The Sheik's Rediscovered Lover
The Tycoon's Defiant Southern Belle

The Sheik's Dangerous Lover (free novella)

The Thorpe Brothers
His Captive Lover
His Unexpected Lover
His Secretive Lover
His Challenging Lover

The Sheik's Defiant Fiancée (Free Novella)
The Prince's Resistant Lover (Free Novella)
The Tycoon's Make-Believe Fiancée (Free Novella)

The Friendship Series
The Billionaire's Masquerade
The Russian's Dangerous Game
The Sheik's Beautiful Intruder

The Love and Danger Series – Romantic Mysteries
Intimate Desires
Intimate Caresses
Intimate Secrets
Intimate Whispers

The Alfieri Saga
The Italian's Passionate Return (Novella)
Her Gentle Capture
His Reluctant Lover
Her Unexpected Admirer
Her Tender Tyrant (December, 2014)
His Expectant Lover (January, 2015)

The Sheik's Intimate Proposition